Island of Lies

A Novel

Pamela Laux Moll

Island of Lies

A Novel by

Pamela Laux Moll

Copyright ©2015 by Pamela Laux Moll
First paperback edition © November 2015 by Pamela Laux Moll
Printed in the United States of America
www.pamlaux.com
ISBN: 978-1-892357-01-4
Beau Ridge Publishing

In memory of my dad, a Navy man.

∞∞∞∞∞∞∞∞∞∞

To Kyle

∞∞∞∞∞∞∞∞∞

ACKNOWLEDGEMENTS

∞∞∞∞∞∞∞∞∞

I am indebted to the following people for their contributions to this book. To my street team of beta readers for their insights to making the story better: Jennifer Collins, Connie Gates, Natalie Nicodemus, Tamera Connelly, Diane McPhearson, Jodeen Simmons, Marilyn Neal, Jay Falconer, Christine Nikles and Kyle Moll.

To all of my family and friends for their encouragement and support that assisted me through the journey, from the bottom of my heart, thank you.

To Lissa, for her advice on a major turning point in this story.

To my dad, Ferris Gates, for letting me know, "I could do anything I wanted."

To my three kids, Lissa, Ben, and Courtney Laux — and my stepsons, Tyler and Brandon Moll.

No man is an Island... he is a peninsula.

John Donne, modified by Jefferson Airplane

One

RYLEIGH STIRRED AWAKE by the sound of slapping waves and the heavy, dead weight of the naked body practically lying on top of her. She wondered how long she had been out. After a few nudges from the top of her head, she was released from his grasp. She shook her pins-and-needles arm. The dry cracks in her lips stung from the saltwater and the gritty sand stuck to her matted chestnut hair. She covered her mouth, fighting back an acute feeling of nausea.

Flocks of wading birds took flight from the shallow strip of land. The sandbar jutted out of the turquoise water, surrounded by lush green islands, blossoming in every direction. Several of the neighboring islands surrounded the sandbar with only a few football fields' worth of space between them, making them all resemble one large island.

The sky grew dark, and the wind picked up. She sat up admiring him. Their sweat, and love aromas, still hung in the island air, filling her nostrils and titillating her hunger for him all over again.

"Elliot." Ryleigh brushed her hand over her lover.

After a few seconds, his eyes fluttered open. "What, babe?" Elliot gazed through bloodshot, aqua eyes, determined to focus on her face, but his eyes shifted to her body. "Well, hello there, naked goddess."

"We need to swim back to Keg Key. We've been here a while. The sea looks rougher than when we got here." Ryleigh wasn't sure how long they had been asleep, but she estimated that if they were to make it back to the group, before the storm brewing overhead exploded, they needed to get going.

Their slumber had come easy, with their being sated from their passionate lovemaking, combined with the exhaustion from the swim to the tiny strip of land, the relaxing surrounds and the fruity rum punch they had consumed on the excursion boat passage from the cruise ship. She had finally relaxed with no concerns about being trailed or followed, like she worried about back home in Chicago. This was a much needed vacation.

"We should head back.

"Not yet," Elliot pouted. "We haven't even explored that sandbar over there with the small palm tree."

"There's a storm coming." She pinched his nipple.

"Ouch. Can't we wait a little and swim to that sandbar? It would be such a pity to go back just when we discovered all these tiny private islands."

"But if there's a storm, we wouldn't be able to swim to that sandbar anyway."

"Now wouldn't that be wonderful," he snuggled up against her. "We could stay here forever."

She couldn't argue with a romantic like that, could she?

"Relax, lay down with me, for a few more minutes?" He grinned, showing a beautiful smile, one that had held her gaze the first day they had met, thirteen months earlier. "I want every minute with you to last."

He leaned toward her, and took her mouth. Slow and smooth, no rush or urgency. Earlier, they had made love on the sandbar like giddy teenagers, high on exhaustion and rum punches.

She liked that Elliot was a little controlling, in a good way, so different from other men she knew. Ryleigh laid her hand across his chest as she pulled away from him. "I'm ready to go. We can't be late." In her mind, they should have left sooner.

He stared appraisingly at her, smiled crookedly, and winked. Then his heavy eyes fluttered as he rolled on his back, sprawling in all directions.

"I'm going to convince you," she said, as she laid her head on his chest, "with my tongue."

"Aw, private island utopia."

"Shhh. Don't worry," she whispered in his ear, "once we're back on the main island and hook up with all the other couples, you'll still have all my attention." She really wanted to leave the sandbar. And it was true, this sexy man, Elliott Finn, could have all her attention for the rest of the cruise, but then what? Where would she go when the cruise ended? When would they be together again?

"I do want you all to myself." He rolled on his side, pulling her to him. His impossibly blue eyes searched her face. "We'll be fine. Just relax a few more minutes, okay?" He hugged her, making no attempt to play or to leave.

There under the dark clouds hiding the sapphire skies, with only the emerald water surrounding them, his insatiable passion and his unquenchable desire burst.

Ryleigh exhaled, and slid back down flat on her back, sluggishly, as her breasts flattened just the tiniest bit beneath their own heavy weight. Normally very modest around Elliot, she felt comfortable *au naturel*. She was thirty-two years old and had never experienced sunbathing in the raw. It was sparkling. And there wasn't another soul in sight for miles. Even if other cruise passengers had made their way to the other side of the island, they wouldn't be able to see them from shore without high powered binoculars.

A passing seagull fought the wind above them, and there was a smell of sea grass and crushed conch shells, and the salty tang of the sea. All new aromas to her, the city girl.

Elliot spooned up against her, murmured something inaudible, and then closed his eyes.

He couldn't be that exhausted. They had just swum out this far. Plus, it was Elliot who had insisted they drink rum punches as a celebration of their first cruise together. Ryleigh had a secret celebration of escaping the troubles she'd left behind. Ryleigh, as a rule, addressed her problems head-on and faced the issues they brought her. But this situation with her company was out of control, and she needed time to think.

"Okay then, just fifteen more minutes," she yawned, like she had a choice. She didn't want to swim back without him. It was a slightly overcast day, with dirty cotton ball clouds bunched up on the near horizon, enough to worry her.

She hoped they'd be on the cruise ship before the rain and in time to get a manicure. She couldn't wait to take a hot shower, and possibly the longest bath of her life. She felt sand in every crevasse of her body.

She didn't want to be late, and in her corporate world, she never was. To her colleagues and superiors, Ryleigh Agatha Lane was always in control, no matter what happened in her personal life and no matter how out-of-control her business life had gotten at Dexco Pharmaceuticals.

She came from a structured world, and as hard as she tried, a vacation didn't always fit that mode. Uncomplicated routine ran in her blood. Her great grandfather, on her father's side, had come from a small mountain town in Italy. She had visited the tiny Italian town, and fallen in love with her ancestors' farm village, their modest lifestyle, and the mountain views straight from *The Sound of Music*. Ryleigh had doggedly sought answers about her family's origins after her parents' accident.

Ryleigh watched, in the distance, bony streaks of lightning explode into tiny electric rivulets.

She shivered. "Elliot, we need to swim back. Look! A storm is heading this way."

"Hmmm," he answered. His hair was wet from the increasing tide reaching their spot, and flakes of sand glittered in his golden sideburns.

Why is he purring and not waking? The thought nagged her. "It's time to go now. I can swim back without you, but I'd rather you come with me. "

He didn't open his eyes and his snores were loud, like those of an oblivious drunk.

"Elliot Finn! Come on. Aren't you concerned? I'm ready to leave," she said as sweat dribbled down her neck. She tried to determine the approximate time. It could be two or two-thirty, but it would take a few hours without dilly-dallying to get back. The excursion ferry boat would leave Keg Key promptly at five. Maybe the storm would veer off to sea and die well before it reached the uninhabited island. She leaned over him and shook him, but Elliot rolled over on his stomach, making no attempt to wake up.

TWO

FROM WHERE RYLEIGH SAT on the sandbar, she searched the palm lined beach for any sign of another passenger. She came up with nothing.

Earlier that day, their walk to the other side of the excursion island had taken them over an hour. Once on the deserted beach, Ryleigh had bent down often, collecting powdery sand dollars like they were treasured doubloons. Elliot had convinced her to wade out in ankle deep water, and only then had they seen the sandbar and decided to swim to it.

She had protested, and not wanted to swim the distance, but the truth was, Ryleigh was there for an all-out-needed escape. Secrets and lies had left her guilt-ridden. She had searched for a means of getting away – the uninhabited island was a temporary solution, but still a means to that end.

The sapphire blue water, powder white sand, and green-covered coral rocks collided around the island like an abstract expressionist painting coming undone.

Ryleigh grabbed his hand and squeezed it. "Elliot, sweetheart, wake up. You're missing the beautiful views. And it's time to go back." She inhaled and felt her nostrils flare as she tried to retain her mounting worry. *Enjoy the view. Enjoy the private island.*

"Okay, three more minutes," he murmured.

She searched Elliot's khaki swim trunks that were tossed on the sand near him for his running watch, but came up empty.

On their way over on the ferry boat, an announcement had blared overheard, *"Remember to return to the ferries by five o'clock. See the attendants in the tiki hut for snorkeling gear, beach volleyball, fishing poles, and other beach games. Lunch will be served at noon."*

Ryleigh and Elliot had missed lunch, and she was starving and thirsty. She wished she had worn her large straw hat tied with her new blue Fendi scarf. She'd only brought her turquoise bikini with rhinestone trim on their sandbar getaway, and it now lay scattered on the sand next to her. She had left her white jean shorts adorned with angel wings on the lawn chair at the beach with her driver's license still in the back pocket.

"Elliot." She leaned over him and kissed his shoulder, then his neck. "Wake up!"

"Hmmm." He moaned. "Ms. Bossy."

Before he could fall back asleep, she grabbed his hand. "This has been awesome, but we need to return now. I'll leave without you," she whispered in his ear.

Elliot mumbled into her hair. "I'm glad you like it. I researched the Keg Key excursion, and knew there were many sandbars connecting all of the atoll of islands, particularly this unoccupied isle ripe for naked adventures... just for us."

Ryleigh knew it had taken Elliot several months of planning to even make the cruise trip possible. But in the end, no one knew they were there. At least not anyone close to either of them. Totally under the radar. Even today, their friendly cruise coordinator didn't know that they had snuck off from the group. If Ryleigh screamed at the top of her lungs, the other vacationers on Keg Key couldn't have heard her.

Hours before, they had waded through several feet of water along the east side of Keg Key. The clear water went up to their chests, at some places, as they ventured over to where the jetty couldn't be seen from the island. They had spotted several sandbars when Elliot saw birds flocking on them about a quarter of a mile offshore.

They had swum side-by-side, lying on their backs and splashing each other with their feet, swimming underwater and even racing each other to the next sandbar where they could stand and rest.

They had giggled and frolicked in the water in places they could wade; other times, they swam and swam.

She had followed closely, and wanted to yell out to Elliot, but she didn't want to admit her fear to him, or herself. He might have stronger muscles, but she was quite an athlete herself.

The currents had carried Ryleigh and Elliot farther out, where the surf was active but not tiring. Ryleigh had treaded water behind Elliot, not realizing until now how far they had drifted and swum. The palm trees on the beach looked like bony fingers on spread-out hands. Ryleigh had never swum this far from shore and she felt an uneasiness in her chest.

From her vantage point, she noticed that the small party island had a few brothers and sister islands, as well. It was a cluster of palm tree lined oases.

They had made love on the thin towel on the sandbar, and she hoped that this was going to be the start of a new chapter in their lives. She also hoped her pale, sunburnt Chicago skin would turn into a luscious tan in a few days.

Ryleigh couldn't believe they had made this part of their vacation come true. They were out of sight from everyone. Not a boat could be seen on the open seas. Not a plane in the skies. Just her and her man.

THREE
The Excursion Beach

LILAH, THE CRUISE coordinator, wandered among the tourists asking them if they were having a good time. She had been in the cruise industry for a dozen years, had a degree in etymology, spoke four languages, and had relatives and friends all over the globe, and still she never got tired of the excursions to remote islands, her favorite part of the cruises she worked.

She stopped and stared at the rain clouds threatening the beaches of Keg Key, littered with passengers from the Ahoy Cruise Ship. The clouds overhead had become a blanket of comfort for many of the German tour groups on the party island. Their fair ivory skin slathered with sunscreen was no match for the sun's burning rays against the white crushed coral sand beaches. Fortunately, her naturally tanned skin rarely burnt under minimum sunscreen.

Trevor, a boyishly handsome 29-year-old, came over to her. He was the Skipper of one of the ferry boats, and bearded and deeply tanned, he looked like an Indian.

"Hey, Lilah."

"Hey, Trevor. What's up?"

"The Captain has asked us to return to the ship. Tropical storms are threatening to hit the entire basin earlier than forecasted," Trevor, the bronzed ferry driver frowned and crossed his arms in front of him. "He wants the passengers back on board. Looks like we're returning to port a day early."

Lilah and Trevor were childhood friends. They had grown up on the islands. They both shared a love for the sea and a hatred for the tourists that they served.

"How does Peter know?" Lilah asked.

Trevor raised his bushy eyebrows at her, "Captain Peter," he said with a futile grin.

"Yes, *Captain Peter*." She was anxious for the day to end, and Trevor's jealousy was evident in his look at her. The early departure news came as an unexpected, but pleasant, surprise. She was traveling to Lisbon the day after the cruise line made port, for a long overdue vacation at her cousins'. Maybe she could catch an earlier flight.

"NEMA said the storm has come up faster than planned," he said, sounding official.

Lilah knew that the National Emergency Management Agency monitored the weather activity and sent out their observations of changing patterns way before the local weatherman knew.

"The storms will travel from the leeward and windward islands, east of Snake Isle and Maldonado."

"Really?" Lilah felt her eyebrows rise. "That's quite a stretch. I'll start gathering the passengers. How long 'til we take off? We have a lot to pack up this time."

"I'm not sure there'll be time to pack everything as we were told. I have orders to leave now."

"Yeah, the new parent company won't use this excursion island."

Trevor looked at the tiki hut and back at the woods leading to the center of the island, and then back to the ocean. "Too bad. It's been a beautiful stop over the years."

"Yes, but the bugs and snakes are getting out of control." With her knowledge of the cruise industry, she'd known the excursion to this outpost island wouldn't last long. As it was now, the cruise ship stopped at another larger island in the atoll, then ferried the passengers to Keg Key, the remote island they stood on. The larger island stop was a crude one for the cruise ship to anchor.

The cruise liner had difficulty getting into the channels around the islands, so it moored offshore, and tenders pulled it to a small dock with a rickety aluminum ramp for the passengers to debark on. The largest island in the group where the Royal Ahoy Liner anchored was set up as the cruise ship port. Only RAL stopped there. Once on the main port island, passengers could spend the day shopping at the kiosks set up just for the passengers, lounge on a beach on the main island, or take an excursion to Keg Key.

"You don't like the bugs and rats? Since when? I've known little Lilah since we were in diapers. You were always catching little critters."

"And you liked to catch turtles."

"Jedd caught the turtles."

Jedd was always at Trevor's side. His loyal chow. He wasn't with him today because they were working.

Thunder crackled overhead, and Lilah turned toward the rippling electric clouds. "There's our cue to get going."

"Let's gather everyone on board. We're looking for two hundred and fifty-seven souls on board in less than an hour. Can you manage that?" If Trevor was concerned, there wasn't a hint of it on his face. With all their combined cruises, this was the first time that either of them had departed the island before five o'clock.

"I'll have Simon and Chaz help me with the head count." Lilah kicked a small black snake into the brush and looked at Trevor, faking a scary grin. The snakes were notorious on the island, another reason the cruise line had decided to abandon it. Too many complaints.

"Harmless," she said, and focused her eyes to the overcast sky where heavy grey clouds floated ominously overhead. She bit her lip and then gave a brief nod.

Trevor had a look of proud purpose on his face as he turned back to prepare his boat, but before he left, he reached for her hand

and she took his, squeezing so tight it was almost painful. "Be careful," he whispered.

Lilah smiled a genuine smile at Trevor – she couldn't help it; she was actually happy he was there to guide them back over the rough waters. She watched him walk away for a few moments. His khaki cruise-line hikers came to rest above his knobby-kneed legs. He wore the same cap as Lilah, but with a captain's emblem, signifying his pilot's job on the ferry boat. He rubbed the scrubby brown beard that encircled his strong, tan face and open smile. The Aston family had been boating for three generations around the islands off Wahoo Key. Trevor Calhoun Aston III stopped to talk to a few passengers, but not before glancing back at Lilah and winking at her.

FOUR

IT TOOK three cruise directors, plus the beach grill cook and the cleaning staff, to get the word out quickly to everyone on the beach. Lilah could tell their early departure news had lost something in translation because of the scurrying of the passengers. The beach emptied quickly as the beachgoers gathered up their belongings and began lining up to board the ferry.

Lilah saw two college-age girls standing by the lawn chairs, gathering their belongings.

"Hurry up ladies, grab your stuff, we're losing time. Sorry to rush you, but we have a storm to beat."

"Arrie, get the hat," the taller girl said.

The young girl grabbed the hat, and when she did, a paperback book and a wad of clothes fell out from under it. "Cool," the girl said, and tossed the paperback back on the chair and unfolded the clothes. "Look at these shorts, they're designer." She held a pair of white shorts with angel wings on the back pockets.

"Is that your stuff?" Lilah yelled at them.

"What stuff?"

"The shorts and hat."

"No, madam."

"Okay, there's no one left on the beach to board. Can you please bring it and turn it in to lost and found?"

"Yes, madam."

"Thanks. Now get going."

"Aye, Aye, Captain." The taller girl saluted Lilah, and the girls giggled and scrambled off toward the ferry.

Lilah made two checks on her notepad. The sky became darker and darker as the addled passengers wandered toward the ferry boats.   The beach was empty in less than thirty minutes as the confused and nervous tourists lined up to board the two ferries.

Lilah concentrated, her index finger bouncing back and forth, as she counted heads on the ferry boat. She returned to the line and recounted, starting with a family of three. She jotted three checkmarks in the columns on her notepad. One male, one female, one child. She went down the list, checking off people in line.

At the front of the line, a young boy whispered something in his mom's ear.

"Now?" she said to him.

The little boy shook his head quickly, with wide eyes, and then stuck his hand between his legs. The young boy's hefty mother pulled his arm and dragged him over to the closest port-a-potty.

Simon, the young cook, raced up to Lilah as she stood in front of Trevor's ferry. "This line includes one hundred and ninety passengers," Simon reported back, huffing between breaths.

"Thanks. The smaller ferry is boarded and ready to depart for the cruise ship. Last count showed sixty-four passengers." Lilah did a quick calculation in her head. "We're missing three passengers?" Lilah's face bunched up in puzzlement. She was wearing her official Ahoy Cruise line baseball cap with her short dirty blonde ponytail poking through the back strap. She lifted it off her head and absentmindedly scratched her hair as she looked at her clipboard again.

Another lightning bolt produced a thunderclap that sounded like a bomb.

"It's getting closer. Let's get going." Lilah saw a German lady and her small son come out of the port-a-potties. Had she counted them? "That should do it." She pointed toward the makeshift bathrooms, at the mother and son. A titanic gust of wind came up suddenly, and with hurricane force, everything not tied down became airborne. She watched as the woman's maxi skirt wrapped around her white, tree trunk ankles, keeping her from walking properly.

Lilah grabbed Simon's extended arm to hold her own balance.

"That should be your missing three?" Simon shouted over the roaring wind, as he looked at the smaller ferry and pointed at a man standing with his hands on his hips, at the end of the gangplank and waiting for his maxi-skirt-tied wife, now yanking her son's extended arm, to join him. Still holding Lilah in place, Simon grabbed the railing to steady himself as she watched him brace against the wind's swells.

"Yeah. Let's secure the hut." Lilah yelled over the wind. She held onto her cap as she looked at the sky. Dark clouds were boiling up from out of nowhere, stitched together with sparkly threads of lightning. *Here it comes.*

She hastily helped Simon secure the hut. The two were locking the thatched door when the winds forced every palm tree and every plant forward, waving and creaking, and rubbing their branches against the hut. Several coconuts fell, making a popping sound as they hit the sand and water.

"Too bad we couldn't crate up anymore of the supplies."

"The cruise line will send someone to pack up all of the remaining stuff." He shouted.

"Agreed. Let's go," Lilah yelled back. The two ran toward the boats. "Crap." She suddenly stopped.

"Now what?"

"I think you forgot your duffle bag." She turned back. "I saw it behind the hut." The sand swirling around them temporality blinded their view of the hut.

Simon checked his pocket, and pulled out his cell and wallet. "Screw it."

15

"Aren't you going back to get it?" Lilah frowned up at the sky.

"No, just a change of clothes and magazines."

"I can have Trevor grab it later," she shouted to him.

"No, really, it's nothing at all."

They were the last two on board Trevor's ferry.

On the ferry's voyage back to the cruise ship, the passengers did not receive rum punches, there were no bands playing calypso music, and the scene was somber as all eyes stayed glued to the sky. Silently, they watched the gathering storm. There was an unsettling feeling in the air.

"Everyone, move downstairs!" Lilah yelled to the passengers on the upper deck.

All passengers crowded tightly together on the lower deck of the larger ferry, bracing against the wind. Lilah felt the first raindrops hit her cheek like fat exploding tears. Then hundreds of warm pellets peppered her face and shoulders. Raindrops bounced off the teak, tungsten-oiled seats, changing the color grains and making them slick. She prayed there would be no use for the moldy lifejackets under the seats.

Everyone looked worried when the ferry leaned over on the starboard side. Many passengers cried out as they scrambled quickly under the covered deck, like a feisty bunch of fire ants scurrying when their mounds are kicked.

Lilah stared through the rain with blurred vision, and then before she knew what had happened, a forceful wind knocked her clipboard from her hands, tumbling it into the swirling sea. Empty-handed, she resolutely moved toward the covered deck.

FIVE
The Sandbar

AFTER A FEW moments of sleeping, Elliot sat up disoriented like he had so many times before. *What city was he in? What hotel? What day was it?*

He remembered. He was right where he wanted to be. There was no other place like this island in the world. Just a sandbar away from the remote island hidden away, an over 12,000-acre oasis of tranquility. Trees, hills, azure seas, caves, hidden treasures, privacy; a plethora of the right ingredients for their escape.

A hefty gust of wind rushed by them. It had the refreshing fragrance of the ocean. Elliot inhaled the air – it was much fresher than Florida. He loved the feeling of the burn from the tropical sun mixed with the itch of salt drying on his skin.

"Hey, gorgeous," Elliot squeezed her hand as it rested in the sand. He noticed she had put her tiny bikini back on. "Are you expecting company?" They had always talked about sleeping out in the open, on a beach, in the nude. The cruise, so far, had fulfilled many of their fantasies, and yet he still had other surprises for her.

"No, I was ready to leave. I don't want to swim back nude."

"I agree with you, we need to swim back, but I disagree on the nude part," he said while glancing overhead, then smiling back at her.

The sandbar had taken on quite a bit of water, and the tiny strip was now diminished down to being a few feet across. The clouds hovered over the other side of Keg Key and many of the small surrounding islands where rain was already falling.

"Wow, where did our private island go?" Ryleigh murmured, sporting a worried frown on her face.

"The tides are changing as the day continues." He watched the heavy rain clouds that were moving higher and closer together, assembling themselves into fantastic shapes that seemed alive.

"Are you up for the swim back? I hate this, but we should get going."

She nodded.

Elliot threw on his trunks, but left the towel in the sand. "I'm not taking that back with us."

"I agree. I hate polluting the pristine sandbar, but you don't want that extra weight on your shoulders. We can come back for it on our next trip here."

He smiled, knowing they would never come here again. Her maybe, but not him. "Ready?" He stood at the edge of the sandbar.

"We're going that way." Elliot pointed in the direction he knew to be the excursion island.

They walked out as far as they could, until it was time to get horizontal and swim toward the party island.

They had only been swimming for a few minutes when he heard Ryleigh scream, "Shark!"

SIX

Where was she going?

He swam to her on the sandbar. "What happened?" He snapped sharply, surprised.

"There!" She pointed out to the horizon. Just as she said the words, he saw two dolphins fly out of the water, chasing one another. He rolled his eyes and gave her a crooked grin of resignation. *Women.*

"Oh." She covered her mouth. "Sorry, Elliot. I thought it was a shark. I swear I saw a dark fin. I'm from Chicago; we don't have dolphins in Lake Michigan." She tried to cover up her concern, but she still had a fearful look in her eyes.

"Come on. We really need to get going." He gave her a squeeze on her arm. He looked at the sky, feeling nervous that they might not make it before the storm. *Just great. Perfect timing.*

"Do you think they would come pick us up?"

"I don't think the ferry boat will come to this side. We haven't seen a boat in this cove of islands all afternoon. Let's go." He squeezed her hand. "Ready?"

Waves and sudsy ocean streams broke over the crown of the sandbar and melted into the ocean, leaving the shore appearing farther out from earlier and now their standing ankle-deep on the hidden beach created a daring sense of separation from the rest of the world. Elliot could see the worry in her eyes.

"I've been ready to get back, even if it means a swim in the rain and storm. I'm ready when you —" She didn't finish her sentence. The rain tumbled down from the tumultuous clouds that had turned from gray to black, and very quickly. "Are you sure it's alright to swim now?"

The storm moved over them, the winds increased, and the rain hit hard.

"As much as I hate to say this, it is probably smarter to wait it out here on the sandbar." Elliot felt it was safer to withstand the hazards of staying put on the small piece of land than to jump into the unknown grasp of the rough waters and take the risks.

"Hopefully, it's a quick storm and it will move through." Windy, sideways rain drenched them more than the sea had, and then the sky broke open and everything came out.

Pelting rain assaulted their bare shoulders. Elliot saw a vast, dark, solid curtain in a solemn movement from the heavens to the sea, moving swiftly toward them. He put the large towel over their heads to keep the sand from flying in their eyes. They crouched under the towel, huddling close to each other. The storm's darkness loomed above them like a sheet pulled over a dead man's face.

The torrent of water surrounded them in every direction, making the thin towel no match for the burst of waves splashing on them.

Several waves crashed and sputtered over the area where they sat, leaving them in a few feet of water; forcing them to scoot along the sand on their bottoms, like two snails, until they found higher ground. They crisscrossed the tiny sandbar.

Through the thin towel, Elliot could see the flashing all around them. The fierce storm rattled over their heads for what seemed like hours as the lightning zigzagged across the sky.

He now worried that the swim to the sandbar might have been a mistake, or was that an added vantage – to spend more time here?

Ryleigh's trembling body pressed up against him. He remained calm. He had participated in plenty of tumultuous events in his life, and being stranded in a storm was nothing to him. He just couldn't tell Ryleigh about it, not yet. Some lies were meant to protect people, even those he cared about deeply.

A white flash of lightning burst over their heads. Ryleigh dug her nails into Elliot's arm and buried her head in his chest. The thunder ripped through his ears with its jagged sound. It crashed and splintered against them as it shook. It felt close as it continued to split the sky wide open to let the rain pour down on them. Ryleigh flinched at every thunderclap.

As quickly as the storm had come in, it slowed to a purr.

"Are you okay?" Elliot whispered in her ear.

She glanced at him and her face was like a ghost, startled and shaken with fear. "I think so." She took the towel off her head. "Shit! That was the scariest thing I've ever done. Oh my God! I think I peed my swimsuit, but who would know it? We're soaked!"

"I thought I felt warmth run over my legs." He grinned at her. "That was rough."

Her face went from a smile to a frown. "Do you think they are headed back to the cruise ship yet?"

"I'm worried, they may have already gone back."

"What? But it's too early. I mean, I really don't have any idea what time it is, but it seems like it has to be close to five. And they wouldn't leave without us, would they?" Her voice was panicky.

"No. They probably took a few of the passengers back that wanted to return to the ship. They have several ferry boats. We'll just swim back and meet up with other stragglers, and catch the later ferry."

Even though the storm had left the seas rough, they both agreed to swim back right away before the last ferry left Keg Key. Elliot just hoped they could make it back in time.

SEVEN
Ahoy Cruise Ship

THE LARGE FERRY rolled violently as Lilah watched Trevor maneuver it closer to the cruise ship. Many passengers screamed. Lilah felt battered as the wind and rain hit her. She adjusted the brim of her ball cap, but it was useless; the water dribbled down her face and neck. She watched the surging waters below as they thrashed to port, where the cruise ship sat.

The smaller ferry was unloading the last of its passengers. The first few families on the gangway hefted their beach bags over their shoulders and peacefully entered the cruise ship. But as the sound of thunder clapped like cymbals in succession, the vacationers trudged faster, swaying up the bridge to get into the ship.

A lady shrieked in pain as the boat smashed her ankle and snapped it, colliding against the side of the ship. Lilah watched helplessly while an older man supported her and half-carried her up the gangplank, the lady crying loudly the whole time.

The electronic turnstiles prevented entry until cruise personnel scanned the passengers' I.D. badges. There was a throng of people waiting as the two ferry boats were joined with the other boats returning from the day's excursions.

The sounds of imminent disaster were all around; kids crying, running feet, and the heavy splashes of the waves crashing on the ship's sides. Passengers quickly stampeded the ship's entrance as news spread like a fungus that the ship was hastening to leave to outrun a hurricane. The cruise ship personnel could not hold back the frightened and confused crowds as they rushed for their cabins.

The remaining passengers on the outside passageway pushed forward with growing horror. Even the seasoned Ahoy personnel wore fear on their faces.

"Stop, mister," Lilah shouted from her position at the turnstiles as she watched a family scramble out through the scuttle, and the father jumped over the turnstile, bypassing the I.D. badge scanner process. His anxious wife passed their three young children over the metal barricade to him, and then he helped his wife climb over.

"Go check that out," Lilah said to her colleague.

Many other families followed them. The personnel continued scanning I.D.s in rapid succession while security personnel approached the gate-jumpers.

"Hey Lilah, are all your excursion passengers on board?" the supervisor asked Lilah as he surveyed the mutinous conduct.

"Yes, we returned with two-hundred-and-fifty-seven from both ferries," she replied. "Are we really leaving tonight?" She asked hopefully, dreaming of her vacation a day early.

"Yes, I believe we are at sea after everyone's boarded."

Lilah looked at the crowd that was forming. "Let me stop in my stateroom, change into dry clothes, and I'll come back to handle the aftermath."

He tipped his hat and returned to the crowd.

Within minutes, Lilah closed the cabin door behind her, and pushing her back against it, she slid to a squatting position. The four walls closely surrounding her suddenly made her feel safe. She closed her eyes and leaned against the door, hoping to regain her composure. She wouldn't succumb to the power of her emotions. She stood up and wiped at a tear that slid down her cheek.

EIGHT
The Sandbar

RYLEIGH FELT every inch of her body aching as she battled for air. Warm, heavy waves washed over her head, while sand, seaweed and algae brought up from the storm tore at her bare skin. She searched for air, nibbling for breaths between nauseating gulps of salt water.

Elliot was at her side the whole swim back to Keg Key. Her heaving brought him closer to her. His hand balanced her head as they stopped to catch their breath and floated. Ryleigh caught a mouthful of salty waves and vomited pink bile.

He whispered to her, "Stop chumming for sharks."

"What? Don't tease me. I'm already in a panic." She glanced around the rough waters and back at Elliot. He loomed over her, holding her slightly up, gazing into her face. He looked a bit worried that he'd frightened her.

"Sorry." He treaded water, holding her head above the waves as she floated awkwardly on her side.

"Are you ready? My arm muscles are cramping." His expression looked pained, but not from cramping.

"Okay, I'm fine now. You're better at this than me."

It was true that Elliot was a great athlete. He had told her that he played football in high school, but according to Elliot, it had been his older brother, Ron, who'd rarely been off the sports page during their college years.

Throughout the cruise, Elliot told her he had swum forty laps in the large pool, after pounding out six miles around the promenade deck every morning. He had even hit the fitness room and lifted weights a few mornings while she enjoyed the spa. He was a cinder block of a man, and she was a powder puff of a woman.

Ryleigh looked up and saw the shore. Finally! She could do this. She started swimming again. Time had stood still. *How come the shoreline is not getting closer? Swim, damn it! Swim, Ryleigh Agatha Lane! You can do it. Swim!*

Just when she felt her strokes were getting into a rhythm, she would get hammered with a wave tossing her sideways. They had drifted far off their path. The island seemed so much further away from the sandbar than it had when they had swum out earlier that day.

Ryleigh felt like she was swimming upstream. She swam further away from the sandbar that had been their sanctuary all day, her shoulders and arms tingling with fatigue. The high waves off the sea kept shoving her back, slowing her progress.

She would glance up, every ten strokes, to see Elliot swimming nearby. He was calm, but seemed to be struggling, too. He was in good shape, but he was also six years older than Ryleigh. *Keep swimming.* Think about the spa appointment. Think about the precious massage and pedicure. She had to reach the ferry!

Several times, the strong waves pushed her sideways, but she did not correct her path. She only wanted to reach shore, and she took refuge in the waves carrying her toward land; even if the current was diagonal, it was forward progress.

She lost count of the times she had to stop, to rest her arms and legs, or when her raging pulse rate pounded alarm bells in her head, and her arms shook like she had palsy. She would float for a few seconds and visualize the shore in front of them while the rain and sea dripped off her face, and then once again with her arms stretched out, she would be stroking and slapping the water. *I'm a strong person, I can do this! When will we get there? When will this pounding in my head stop?*

She glanced up and the palm trees lining the shore looked like statues, bent over like Divi Divi trees. The flock of birds once perched on the private island was nowhere to be seen, except for two white birds, out of sync with the group, who seemed lost and as if they were following her and Elliot to shore, as their twisted bodies fought the wind.

She would occasionally lie still, letting the force of the inward waves carry her toward shore. Other times, she kicked and kicked again, and the strain on her upper thighs burned, or was that from jellyfish tentacles swiping her legs, leaving their burning poison? Her eyes were wide open, alert, watching for sharks, watching ahead for Elliot.

Ryleigh kept swimming and praying, blocking out the swirling sea water around her. Her heart pounded, but her breath was raspy. She prayed as she stroked harder and deeper into the water. Thoughts of drowning and dying ran through her, but her prayers kept her moving, and didn't let fear take hold of her. She would not stop swimming.

She thanked God when she felt her long legs scrape the ocean floor, and then she felt Elliot grabbing her. He pulled her the rest of the way onto the beach. She laid on the sand with her arms and legs shaking in spasms.

Crouching on all fours, she lifted her head and looked around the beach. "It looks different."

"What?"

"The beach. It's whiter." Maybe the storm had left the beach ashy from pulverized coral and shells.

"Ryleigh, it's okay. We swam to a different point of Keg Key."

"No, I don't recognize this side. Besides, you were hammered off rum punches when we swam to the sandbar." She searched the surrounding beach. "Where'd our sandals go? We left them here."

"Okay, so we walk to the other side. Let's go." He brushed the sand from his leg.

"Oh damn, Elliot." She balled her hands in tight fists and felt every muscle ache. The swim had left her exhausted. "They have to come find us here." *I bet he thinks I'm such a girl sometimes.* This wasn't what she'd had in mind for her island escape.

"No, we have to go find them. Now, come on, get up."

Is he sure he knows the way? She didn't think Elliot knew, but she kept her tongue still. Ryleigh rolled over and slowly stood up. On wobbly legs, she tried to get her land legs back. She plucked seaweed out of her tangled mane of auburn hair and tossed it on the beach. With dignity, she deliberately brushed the crushed sand flakes off her knees and hands. Her emerald eyes glistened with moisture. "Show me the way home."

Elliot led her down an overgrown trail, deeper into the island brush. A tangle of mangroves lay in their path. Birds squawked overhead. It seemed so surreal.

A snake slithered out from under a pile of vines, causing Ryleigh to release a small scream. Elliott approached the serpent and attempted to pick it up.

"Seriously! What are you doing?"

"It's a black snake. Not poisonous. But it will strike if threatened, so stay clear of it."

"You don't have to ask me twice."

They watched as the snake slithered sideways across their path and into the underbrush.

"We don't have giant snakes in Chicago either. No sharks, no snakes," said a breathless Ryleigh.

"It's only a four-footer, darling. And there are probably snakes there – you just don't see them."

"Well, if there are snakes in the city, I don't think we would have rats the size of cats." She didn't know what was worse.

They walked on as Elliott gave her a rundown of the possible snake species on the island.

Ryleigh was tired, hungry, and hung-over, and her body ached from swimming. Salt water was drying on her skin, leaving it stinging all over. Her lips were parched and cracked.

The sun was slipping slowly behind the horizon when they finally made it to the other side of the island.

"Thank God!" Ryleigh said. "Hey, where's the Tiki Hut?" She looked up and down the desolate beach.

"Over there." Elliot pointed toward the water. He sighed and ran a hand through his golden hair, frowning.

Ryleigh followed his gaze across the short distance of water to another island – Keg Key!

"We swam to the wrong fucking island!" She screamed, and fell on all fours and laughed so hard that she cried.

NINE
Royal Ahoy

THE STORM LEFT many passengers scrambling for their rooms, and there they stayed until dinner. Within an hour, the cruise ship chaos was still unruly, just like the sea.

Lilah, in the ship's baggage room, checked the number of luggage pieces that had been collected from outside her stalwart's staterooms.

"In all of my cruises with the Ahoy Cruise line, I've never experienced such a chaotic day. I'm ready for my overdue vacation." Lilah said to Simon.

"No kidding, "he smiled. "I like your uniform suit."

"Thanks. How many pieces did we count?"

"We have two hundred and four pieces already picked up and another hundred and eight pieces in route to storage," Simon said.

"Do we have any of our staterooms not collected yet?" It always amazed Lilah how much luggage the passengers brought on board the ship for a week-long cruise. She was responsible for one area of the ship, with less than a hundred people, and yet their luggage numbered over three hundred pieces.

"I've asked Trevor to go back and get your backpack, after the storm."

"No, you didn't need to do that." Simon insisted as he left the storage room. "It's not worth it."

*   *   *

Twenty minutes later, two floors above Lilah, in the mid-section of the luxury cruise liner, Simon was loading the last of the luggage and checking on passengers. He approached cabin M12 and loaded two very large suitcases. He knocked on the door.

A fat man in nothing but light blue boxer shorts and black socks opened the door. "Yeah?"

Simon looked at his clipboard and asked, "Mr. Callaghan?"

"Yeah." The portly man eyed the skinny, dark haired man in front of him.

"We wanted to make sure all your belongings are packed and you only have your carry-on, purses, backpack, and small items with you," Simon said in a mechanical voice.

"Yeah, can't you tell?" He pointed at the two large suitcases on the luggage rack.

"Okay, we just wanted to verify." Simon had been told to make sure that either the luggage was picked up or the occupants were in their room to verify the luggage. It had been a confusing day, and the captain had asked for the additional procedure for accountability.

M12's door shut.

"Put some pants on, for God's sake."

He had four staterooms left to go. The second room was unoccupied, but easily verifiable. Rumpled bed. Dirty clothes and a lace bra on the floor. The dresser with women's junk on it. Perfume bottles, bronzer powder spilled everywhere, hair extensions, lipsticks, and a curling iron. Four suitcases piled high in the corner, tagged and ready to go.

He continued down the hallway to M15. He looked at his clipboard; *Ryleigh and Elliot.* He picked up the two small cases that had been left out. He knocked on the door. No answer. He knocked again.

He looked at his clipboard before he made a notation. He took out his master keycard and opened the door.

Simon immediately saw the bed was made. He spotted an open book on the nightstand. "Aw, they're still out."

He took one glance into the bathroom and noticed the towels were still neatly folded, the soap untouched, no watermarks on the sink or vanity, no tissues in the wastebasket, and the shower was dry. It was pretty obvious that the occupants hadn't been back to their room since the maid service earlier in the day. He made a note on his list and he confirmed their luggage pick-up.

He messed up the bed, throwing the pillows and comforter on the floor. He turned on the shower and let it run while he dampened a few towels and washrags. He threw a few Kleenex in the toilet and didn't flush it.

On his way out of the room, he grabbed the open paperback book on the nightstand. He would throw it away on another floor.

Simon hadn't worked for this friend of his cousin's before, but he didn't see any harm in making these two passengers appear checked in from the excursion. And he could use the easy five grand they'd promised him. He would log into the software, like they'd shown him, and make sure Elliot Finn and Ryleigh Lane were on board before departure.

He also hoped Elliot would find the backpack he'd left on Keg Key by the tiki hut with the large knife inside.

TEN

THE ROYAL AHOY CRUISE ship steamed out of the islands earlier than planned, as the weather forecasted for the area had concerned Captain Peter Benson. Earlier that day, he'd worried about the weather on this last voyage, but he'd reluctantly made a choice to go forward with the excursion to Keg Key. He now watched the weather radar in the control room, regretting that decision from ten hours earlier.

Captain Peter reviewed possible routes to avoid the worst of the storm. He had a library of charts and guides to the islands with explicit navigational instructions for safely entering practically every passable harbor in the seas. The exit from the Keg Key islands was a tricky one.

The area consisted of 1200 coral islands stretching for over thirty thousand miles, making it one of the most dispersed atolls in the world. The island they'd visited was one of many in this area. It was nicknamed Keg Key because, when the cruise line had originally started excursions there, they had shipped kegs of wine and beer in in large barrels. The keg barrels had quickly been replaced with plastic bottles, but the name seemed fitting for the island's purposes. In addition, rumors had it that whiskey was made on the islands and shipped in kegs.

There was a slight knock at the door.

"Come in," Captain Benson said.

"I brought you fresh coffee, Peter," Lilah said, putting the cup on the table.

His eyes met hers for a minute. "Thanks." He noticed she had changed from her excursion outfit to her night suit. She had a natural, beautiful confidence about her that intrigued him.

"Are you okay?" His eyes looked down at a scratch on her calf.

"It's fine. I scraped it against the turnstile." She looked around the bridge.

Twenty-two years of rolling seas, basking in the sun, and the pickling effect of straight whiskey made Peter feel much older than Lilah even though he was only ten years older.

He put his arms around her and she took a step back. He rested his hand on hers. Lilah, this beautiful, tan-skinned woman with her mocha-colored braid to the middle of her back, held parts of his heart. He knew the young, island excursion captain, Trevor, also jockeyed for her attention.

"Be careful. It's going to get rough tonight. You may want to make sure the passengers stay put. We're leaving soon."

"So it is true? I'll make the announcement." Lilah put her hand on Peter's forearm. "It's going to be okay, right?"

"I hope so. Will you come back later?" He hoped she would be able to eat with him. He loved her company. "A late dinner?"

"I'll try. There's a lot to do."

"See you after 9?"

Lilah smiled as she slipped quietly out of the Control Room.

A few hours later, Peter was concentrating on his radar screens and watching the front cameras. And without warning, a large wave crashed over the deck, followed by another and another. In all his years of captaining a ship, he had never seen waves this high. He called for his first officer, who was enjoying dinner in the main dining room with celebrity guests.

There were only two safe passages between one side of the north ocean to the other, amidst live coral reefs and sand bars, making navigation problematic enough already.

Rolling thunder boomed from overhead. Captain Peter moved the gears and throttle, and prayed that the staff, the passengers, and Lilah were all safe below.

He leaned over the bulkhead, reviewing all the monitors in front of him. The Royal Ahoy ship's designed draft was twenty-six feet, but she probably sat several more feet below her waterline, loaded as she was with all of the passengers and cargo from the abandoned island.

He reviewed the passage he'd chosen again. He knew that this route, through these seas scattered with hundreds of tiny islands, required concentrated navigation. He pushed a few buttons and backed off on Ahoy's throttle as another wave hit the bow.

He maneuvered the cruise liner a bit, guiding the 952-foot-long ship down the lee slope of each wave and then up the windward slope to the next crest, at which point his visual had been moved temporarily off the water and all he saw was darkened skies.

It was on the third high wave, the largest wave he had ever seen, and following the trough, that he was knocked against the door, feeling glass shattering everywhere and his brain darken; all this gray fuzz appeared behind his eyes and he felt himself getting heavier and heavier, and then everything just went black.

ELEVEN

THE FIRST WAVE crashed the main pool deck, leaving Lilah just seconds to grab a railing to brace herself, while everything on the deck that was unattached started to slide from one side to the other; table, chairs, beer cans, dinner plates. The towels draped on the lawn chairs took on an animated life, flying up one second and flopping over the chairs in the next second.

The passengers grabbed anything stable, any fixed fixtures in sight – the sides of the pool railings, the walls, and each other as the waves swelled each time. Many made their way to the exits to find comfort in their cabins.

The ship creaked and groaned. Glassware from the bar crashed to the floor. Some passengers moaned.

The next wave hit so hard that the band's amplifiers' master power strip was temporarily loosened from the outlet and the music stopped for a few seconds, then restarted.

When the ship heeled again, several passengers grappled for the hand railings on the outer edges of the deck and teenagers gripped the shuffleboard table. Those without a secure item to brace themselves against collided with each other as they made it to the exits. A large German man abruptly rear-ended an American dad and bounced him to the floor. He was trampled on by his son.

"Hey, watch where you're going, idiot." The kneeling man yelled.

Lilah rushed over to help the man.

"Are you okay, sir?" Lilah tried to lift him. In the background, she heard the band as they packed up their equipment.

The crowd quieted and everyone looked frightened when the ship leant over on her starboard side. The ship continued to oscillate until it came to a rest after the massive wave passed. More plastic glassware had fallen from the bar, leaving one of the stewards in search of a dustpan.

"The unusual movement in the sea makes it necessary to suspend the party." An announcement blasted out over the microphone. The disappointed passengers staggered to the exits, and many complained and whined as they left the deck.

The passengers began to talk at once.

"Shit, the boat can't tip over like the Poseidon, can it?"

"Did the Titanic hit high waves, too?"

"No, it hit an iceberg."

"The sky is as dark as I've seen it today. Hopefully, this will soon pass."

A burly man grabbed the arm of the cruise line's Master of Ceremonies, the host of the parties throughout the cruise, as he walked by. "Are we in any danger?"

"No, I've seen bigger ships that have leaned until the water was over the second floor port windows. Large waves are common in these seas this time of year."

Lilah thought that if she could have seen behind the sunglasses of the man, she would have seen his eyes wide with fear.

"How far are we now from land?"

The MC glanced at his watch, as if to see the answer there, "We should make landfall by tomorrow morning."

"The wave was spectacular," another passenger said.

"Everyone, please return to your cabins," the announcement repeated.

Two decks below, several young adults were sitting around the lower bar, ignoring the announcement to return to their cabins.

The water crashed, knocking over their bar stools, breaking windows, and soaking everything in its path. The waves smashed out windows in the public area on deck 5, on the forward part of the vessel.

The massive waves hit one right after the other, crashing into the ship like thunder. The damage was done by the second and the third waves. The waves exceeded 30 feet in height. As the wall of water crashed around the college kids, they all went scrambling and screaming. The bar tables were broken off the deck and went over the side, carrying the bar stools and the kids along with them. The waves stirred up with the fierce winds seized everything, and the deck's pool became one and the same as the wild sea.

A straw hat with a blue Fendi scarf wrapped around it still floated in the air, moments after the girl wearing it had been sucked out to sea.

TWELVE
Keg Key

STUPID. Incredibly fucking stupid. There was no other way to describe what he was doing as Trevor stared at the purple-covered map in front of him on his iPad. He enlarged the image, but it still showed purple, hurricane-like weather everywhere in his vicinity. What was he thinking? Could Simon's backpack and a few supplies be worth his and Jedd's lives? But Lilah had asked him to grab them.

He had ditched the ferry for a speedboat. He cruised at 40 knots, inching slowly back to Keg Key after the storms had subsided, not listening to the alerts about the new set of storms headed his way. He planned to retrieve Simon's backpack and load some of the remaining food onto his boat before heading back home for a few weeks of R & R. He was familiar with the islands in the area, and this confidence overweighed sound judgment.

Trevor's father was a sea captain; his grandfather, a sea captain; and his great-grandfather had been a fisherman. At any rate, as far back as his family tree could be traced, all of the men had been intimately connected with the great watery waste.

Lilah, like his mother, loved the sea, too. That was one of the many things that attracted him to her. His mother had often gone to sea with his dad on his long voyages, and so he and his brother had spent the greater part of their childhood upon the water. Thus it was, he thought, that he had come to inherit his love for the sea.

The island from which he'd come slowly faded from view as Keg Key came into sight.

Trevor slowed the boat and Jedd, Trevor's chow, looked anxiously over the edge of the boat and batted at his reflection in the water, and pranced nervously up and down the deck.

"Yeah, I know, really stupid. The storm is coming up fast." His faithful friend stopped, cocked his head at Trevor, and barked.

"Come here, Jedd." Trevor tossed a small fish resembling a sardine from the cooler at the dog.

Jedd caught it in midair.

"Good boy." He turned toward the island. "Lilah was right. You and I are the best and most loyal friends that ever sailed together on the stormy sea. Let's just hope I'm right about the weather patterns and we have plenty of time to get back."

As he approached the southern extremity of Keg Key, the weather became eerie and the ominous skies threatened once again to unload water.

He looked at the navigational app on his iPad. The party island was set amongst a series of a half dozen small islands. The sea tumbled to the east of Keg Key and a brush, tropical island lay to the west side. The other side formed a salt water creek, commonly called Snake Channel, between the bordering islands. There were many legends on how snakes had come to live on the island, but it didn't matter to Trevor. The snakes, along with feral cats, helped keep the mice and rats in control.

The channel entrance would be the calmer choice to reach the tiki hut beach, unless the mushy bog was swollen. Beyond the creek harboring the snakes, which ran a half mile across, was another small island with a dense overgrowth of greenery, nicknamed Brush Island.

Trevor slowly maneuvered his boat toward the channel opening, but decided against that entrance.

He decided to avoid the shortcut, knowing its swollen creek after the storms would be dangerous. He turned and cruised toward the excursion side of Keg Key, directly away from the open sea.

The image on his map showed that Keg Key resembled a barbell from the sky. The ferry boats deposited the vacationers on the lower half of the barbell, closer to the wide open sea.

Trevor had been around this bank of islands a dozen times, and most times, he cruised onto them gently in a warm, tropical breeze, floating calmly on the glassy waves and avoiding the sandbars. Today was different. The storm's squalls had left the sea rough. He had been told by Captain Peter to wait a few days before attempting to go back to Keg Key. But he didn't take his orders from Peter. Especially not Captain Peter, who probably got his advice from watching the weather channel. He hadn't agreed with letting the passengers go on the excursion today. At least they were all safe back on the cruise ship, including Lilah.

He looked at his iPad again and the whole area was covered with purple. "Well, Jedd, I hope they're all safe and sound."

Women. They were so confusing at times. Lilah said she needed time. And perhaps Trevor should step away, he thought, and give her some space. She was going away to Portugal for a month, so it would be easy for him to leave the ball in her court for now. He wouldn't allow himself to close that door and open it for another guy.

By the time he reached the edge of Keg Key, he had made a decision: he would fight for Lilah. She was worth it and they had been through too much together for him to lose her to the likes of Captain Peter, or to lose her at all.

THIRTEEN
Brush Island

AN OCEANIC breeze swept up behind them, fluttering the nearby palm trees, and Elliot watched as it almost knocked one weak, knobby-legged Ryleigh to the sandy beach.

Elliot came to her side and wrapped an arm around her waist. "Come on, Ryleigh, I think it's this way." Clasping her hand, he pulled her body into a warm embrace.

"You've been saying that for the last few hours." She gazed at him for a moment like he was some kind of lost warrior. But she let him, once again, carefully direct her toward the opening in the brush.

"The way these islands seem laid out, is that they're all really connected. Based on my calculations earlier, we had already made our way across the width of the lower part of the island."

"When?"

"When we swam out to the sandbar. I guess, during the storm, we got disoriented, when our sandbar took on new shapes. While we swam in the high waves and rain, we were being pushed farther to the east, toward the tip of the furthest edge of the top of the island."

"Elliot, you really don't know, do you?" She took a big breath, as if winded from their walk.

"From our vantage point at the sandbar, and in the pouring rain, the hourglass-shaped island appeared to be two small separate islands, but they're connected."

Based on his calculations, they had been left behind on Keg Key when they had ventured to the northern tip of the lower half, where the narrow sandbar had formed. They had swum to the top

41

half of Keg Key, where the two halves were only connected by a spinal cord of land.

They had finally made it to the north of the top half of Keg Key, where they'd discovered a small channel between another separate, but smaller, island. That channel had been packed with cord grass and snakes, squeezing the passage to the dense island even more narrowly. Elliot knew from his research on the cruise's voyage that the small inlets and fjords were so numerous in this part of the sea that many didn't have names.

"We're getting close–"

"–Ahhh!" Ryleigh gasped. "Another one!" She jumped behind Elliot as a small black snake about the size of a garden hose slithered across their path.

"What did I tell you?"

"You said the black ones eat insects, and they're okay, not poisonous, and they will leave me alone," she said between heavy sighs.

"Yep, that's right." Elliot grabbed her hand, took the lead, and she followed closely behind him, never taking her eyes off each step she took. He knew Ryleigh would quickly learn to tell the difference between a poisonous snake and a friendly species.

The early night sky made it somewhat difficult to navigate, but Elliot knew that a man with his background had all the qualifications to get them back to the tiki hut safely without disasters. He just had to do it without letting Ryleigh know. He had already identified numerous foliage, and insects, and warned her about snakes, blaming his knowledge on the fact that he'd been a science nut growing up. A simple lie.

He knew Ryleigh, a city dweller, would probably blow her nose on a poison ivy leaf while devouring the deadliest of wild berries. He would have a lot to teach her if they were ever trapped on a deserted island.

42

Time was against them. He knew the storms were returning, and more importantly, the shroud of darkness would make their rescuers more unlikely to see them on the shoreline.

That's when he saw them. Lights. Boat lights.

FOURTEEN

TREVOR's BOAT glided closer to shore as the text message popped up on his iPad. He clicked the message open and his eyes began to sting when he read it.

S.O.S. Mayday, Ahoy Cruise ship is taking on water. Lives may have been lost to sea.

It took him about one second to decide. He turned the boat about-face while in only eight feet of shallow water.

Jedd barked at the island.

"I know, girl, we'll come back someday. But we can't today."

The dog ignored Trevor and kept barking.

Trevor turned around to get a last look at Keg Key. Out of the corner of his eye, to the east on Brush Island beach and amongst the enormous forest of mangroves, Trevor thought he saw a shadow. He took out his binoculars to have a better look, but didn't see anything. It was getting too dark.

He raced the throttle to full speed, and aided by the wind at his back, he hoped to be back at port in seventy minutes, where at least there he could monitor the news about the cruise ship. He headed straight for the distant passage that led out between the larger islands, and toward the lower bay and the open sea. The speedboat made the water fly over the deck as he sped along, the waves causing the little boat to rock violently.

"Hang on, Jedd."

The large dog, his ears back, forced several more hefty barks toward the island and then crouched down at his master's feet, studying the little island disappearing behind them.

FIFTEEN

"GO AHEAD. RUN. Elliot, run. I'll catch up with you." Ryleigh's animated voice shrilled as she watched the boat lights approach the island. Her legs were too tired to chase after it. She just hoped Elliot could reach them.

"Go!" She scrambled behind him, trying to catch up. The only sound heard was her own snapping feet in the brambly path. The snakes forgotten. The crackling twigs underfoot unnoticed. Eyes focused ahead as his shadowy shape got fainter and smaller and further from her, making her hair stand up on the back of her neck.

Looking to the west horizon, she saw the purple sky bouncing with the oncoming lights of their rescue boat. "Run, Elliot." *Make it.*

Ryleigh was closer to the sea. She ran after Elliot as fast as her stiff legs could go. She hardly made a sound, just hissing air breathing in and out of her. Dark hair beating down her sweaty back. Her slim calves flexed and heaved as they cramped up. Her side ached as a stitch grew across her middle abdominal wall, moving to her lower left side. *Damn cramps.* Like a contraction, the pain pushed through her core.

A sonic boom of lightening crashed down, and a few coconuts fell from overhead. This had to be one of the most horrific days of her life.

She stood up, squinting at the canopy of tropical foliage overhead. "Seriously?" She felt drained and vaguely abandoned.

She yelled. "ELL-I-OT!"

"Where are you? Wait up!" She kept yelling out.

This is crazy. How can our wonderful excursion have ended so badly? Soon we'll be sitting on the deck drinking margaritas and laughing about the whole incident.

But now, where did he go?

Luckily, more streaks and booms in the sky were lighting her view ahead. She spotted Elliot as he turned left, running toward the sea.

She was running again, with the strong wind on her face and the prickly sandspurs on the trail stinging the bottoms of her feet. She pressed forward, and every few minutes she dodged flying debris as she made her way down the narrow path.

The sun had almost set now, and here and there, she could make out the lights of the approaching boat bobbing on the sea.

She turned toward the sea at the opening where she had spotted Elliot disappear. She was so focused that she didn't hear the crackle of the palm's branches and the assault of something hard on her head, pushing her down to her knees. It felt like a coconut had been shot out of a canon, making a line drive to her head.

Suddenly staring out into the vast darkness, she saw there were no more boat lights, and no more Elliot. *Just another fucking day in paradise.* Everything became a blur, and darkness surrounded her.

SIXTEEN

ELLIOT SURFACED again, and in the moonlit dusk sky, he could see in the distance the dark shadow of the rescue boat, escaping away from him.

"Come back! Damn you! Come back!" He said it in a whisper, feeling guilty as he said the words barely out loud.

There was nothing around him but white caps and the silent dark horizon as he turned and swam back to shore.

Had he given up too easily? Would Ryleigh think he hadn't tried hard enough to reach the rescue boat? He kept watching the horizon, waiting until the boat was gone. Moments before, he had ducked back into the shadows once when the boat stopped and the captain had surveyed the brushy island.

He scanned the shore for Ryleigh. The wind rustled, clawing at the trees, kicking the sand and waves in swirls, and knocking Elliot off balance and back into the waves on his back. He floated there for a second, then rode the next wave to shore.

His adrenaline was racing after chasing the small speedboat. *Why in hell had the captain turned around so suddenly?* With a relieved sigh and a last glance at the dark, empty horizon, he turned his back to the angry sea.

He searched the beach and spotted Ryleigh lying in the sand, further south of him. Palm leaves and chunks of seaweed swept around her, the gurgling sea just inches from where she lay still. Why didn't she look at him?

He felt a surge of panic. He moved so fast, he didn't remember getting out of the water. When he reached the beach, he ran toward her, yelling her name.

Heavily trained, muscled legs running fast to reach her before the stormy waves swept her limp body out to sea.

Geez, Ryleigh, what has happened to you? Look up! Look toward me.

"Ryleigh!" he yelled. But the wind took his voice as he watched the wind threaten to blow her small, slumped body out into the ocean.

The sand wouldn't give way. It was thick and tugged on his bare feet as he ran the length of the beach to her.

"Ryleigh. Ryleigh, look at me."

He quickly turned her over and saw blood running over her face – a lot of blood. Her eyes were shut. Her auburn hair was matted above her left ear. He listened to her heart. Took her pulse. It was beating fast, but it was beating. *Thank God.*

Quickly, he was brushing the bloody sand from her hair and face, and saying a tumble of words as he did so, none of them meaning anything.

With shaky hands, he splashed seawater on her face and wiped the blood away. Her eyes fluttered and she whispered, "Elliot, you throw one hellava party," in his ear.

"Ryleigh. What happened? Baby, thank goodness. I thought, my God, I thought you were... never mind, it doesn't matter. " He felt relief like he had never felt. And he had held death in his hands before. He had lost people very close to him. But this was a new feeling.

"Did you fall?" He held her face, her lovely face. He pulled her to him and hugged her close.

"No, coconut."

"What?"

"A torpedoed coconut flew at me when I was following you. It must have cut me."

"Jesus. Let me see how deep the cut is. How's your head?"

"Boat? What happened to our rescue boat?" Even in the darkness, her emerald eyes looked deep into his.

"Gone. It turned around. I heard a dog barking. I was so close to the edge of the woods, but when I got out into the beach clearing, the man had turned the boat around and was headed away from me. The dog kept barking as I waved my hands, but he never turned around. It was like he'd seen a ghost or something that scared him away."

"No. Noooo!" She buried her head into his chest. "When will they be back? It's late, dark, and I'm hungry. I need a shower, food, aspirin and my bed!"

"I swam toward the boat, but it was too fast, Ryleigh. Too fast."

Waves with gusts of wind were still beating on them. He was still catching his breath, half kneeling in the sand, her face turned up to his, so close. He had not seen this defeated face before. Not in the Ryleigh he knew.

"Come on. Can you stand? I think we should stay here for a while. Let's move toward the brush." He led Ryleigh to a soft sandy spot under low foliage, void of coconuts overhead.

SEVENTEEN

RYLEIGH COULDN'T believe her bad luck. Hurricane-like storms, missed ferry boats, an abandoned rescue, and a head gash from a torpedoed coconut. Hungry and aching all over from the top of her head to her prickle-covered feet, she felt tears forming on the edges of her eyes.

"Elliot." Ryleigh looked at her stranded lover. "Elliot, what are we going to do tonight?"

He blinked into her eyes, and after a few seconds, he said, "Here's the plan. I'm pretty sure I know where we are. We can rest here, and at the first light of dawn, we'll cross the thin channel and we'll get to the tiki hut and wait."

"Sleep here?" She was disappointed, but not despairing.

"I know. I'm hungry and thirsty. And I bet you are, too. I'll get us coconut and fruit. We really shouldn't attempt a walk in the dark over uncharted ground. You're already a mess. And look at it this way, I won't be stealing your covers."

Elliot was a doll sometimes. In the inky blankness surrounding them, she grinned. "We can't be that far. Right? The boat coming back was close to the hut," she said soothingly. "We saw the hut from the other point."

"Yes, but he took another approach than the ferry boats. Our mistake was when we left the sandbar, the current pushed us to the east, and we swam east of the opening at Keg Key. Then we walked further into the brush and came out on the south side, which is correct, but too far east, and we now will have to –""

She wasn't following Elliot, and interrupted his plan of where he thought they were at. "–so let's just walk along the beach 'til we find it. Hopefully, my cell phone is still buried in the bag in the sand where I hid it. Maybe there are other passengers left behind, and food and water." She wasn't too confident on the other people lagging behind. They hadn't seen any when they'd glimpsed the tiki hut from the point of the brushy, snaky island. She prayed her cell phone still had power. The battery drained quickly. "We can call the ship's coordinator, what's her name? Lilah? Lilly? And they'll be back in a flash." Her head felt like a helium balloon floating between her shoulders, and with each nod she felt the knots from the cut in her scalp. She felt her face turned into a grimace, as her hand raised to rub the cut on her head.

"I wish it was that easy. I'm sorry, but I bet your noggin is aching too. Let's rest. We'll have better luck in the morning. This is an archipelago of islands. And we don't really know if the beaches connect."

"What kind of islands?"

"A cluster of islands. I read that in this area there's over 700."

"No freakin' way!"

"I thought you knew."

"No, we sailed at night. I never bothered to look at the map of our trip. So what's between the two islands? Are they connected? This brushy island and the party island, Keg Key?" She felt Elliot knew a lot more than he was sharing.

"I've taken a helicopter over this part of the sea. There's so many islets, and shallow waters, that it's difficult to know which one we are on. I do know that there's fresh spring water somewhere between the two or three islands around here. We may very well be still on Keg Key, but I can't chance the long walk in the dark."

"What, like a river between them?" *When did he take a helicopter? What else hasn't he told me?*

"I can do it, Elliot." But even as she said the words, she felt her head pounding and her ears ringing. "I need shampoo." She ran her hand through her hair.

"Lie down, Ms. Stubborn, will you?"

51

She could be stubborn, couldn't she? Even now on this trip, when she knew she should have told him about her dangerous and possibly deadly situation back home in Chicago, she hadn't yet. *Why? I had opportunities on the cruise ship, many opportunities to come clean.*

Was she falling in love with this man leaning over her, caring for her head wounds? This awesome, sexy man. And wasn't this trip about her coming clean? *No more lies, Ryleigh Lane. What would your mama think, if she was still alive? No more hiding behind lies. Tell him, Ryleigh. Tell him.*

"Shampoo, dry clothes, drugs, cigarettes, Chardonnay, before I tell you."

"Tell me what? Ryleigh, lie down, you're not making sense. And you smoke?"

"They're miserable people. Nasty, egomaniacal shit-heads, they'll do anything for money, fame, the stocks…" she mumbled.

"Ryleigh, who? You're just a little messed up. The head gash probably. And a lack of water."

"They're bad people. I need my Mac-10 pistol…" she rambled on.

"You own a gun?"

"Work, it's a fucking horror show. They want me dea–"

A bird swooped overhead in a tree and made Ryleigh look up, and that's when she saw it. Coming at her fast in the dark. Round, black, airborne.

EIGHTEEN

"ELLIOT! WATCH OUT!"

She jumped up in time to grab at the dark, rubbery mass.

"So where the hell did this come from?" Elliot took the large, dark inner tube with rope handles away from Ryleigh's shaky, sweaty grasp.

He straddled it in the sand and turned it over. There were three initials on it, R.A.L. "This came off the Royal Ahoy Ship."

"Are you sure it 'came off', or was it on the other side of Keg Key for the passengers to tube with?" *Thank God, a distraction. I almost told Elliot. Not yet.*

"No, this isn't a tube for watersports, this looks like the ones I saw on the 5th deck, used for rescues, I believe."

"How did it get here? Do you think that speedboat left it?"

"No. I was watching him and I didn't see him throw anything off."

"It was pretty dark, Elliot."

"It was dusk, and he didn't toss it. It was a man and a dog on a small speedboat. It looked like a Proline 32."

Ryleigh cocked her head at him in the dark, trying to read his face. "How do you know boats from this distance?" These last ten hours alone with Elliot, she'd realized his survival instincts were amazing and his water knowledge accurate. *Who is this island man?*

"I told you, I spent a lot of time at the beach growing up."

She couldn't see his face when he responded because he was examining the tube, but if she could have, she was pretty sure she'd have seen that look in his eyes that he got a lot when she felt he was fibbing to her. *Such a mysterious man.*

Her stomach growled. "Well, if someone was throwing us a line, I wish they would have included dinner with it, too. I'm famished!"

"How's the head? Just stay put. I'll take a little walk and find some edible fruits and berries for now."

Ryleigh's heart fluttered in her chest. After all she had been through today, battling sharks, giant insects, snakes, flying coconuts... why now was she afraid to be left alone? *Obviously, I'm a fool. There's not a soul around.* But the dark forest made her feel like she was being watched. And she was half-naked in the middle of God-knew-where.

"I can come with you," she said quickly, a little too quickly.

"No, that's not necessary, just rest. I'll be back within an hour."

"It'll take that long?"

"Are you worried?"

"Well, yeah. I don't want a bear or an ape to get you."

"Funny girl. This is an island in the middle of the sea. There aren't bears or apes."

"What about natives?"

"Native what?"

Now she was sounding paranoid. "Just kidding, but are there still native wild men living on remote islands?"

"Maybe, but not these. Too many vacationers from the Royal Ahoy Cruise Line have come here. If anything, we'd have to be worried about drug dealers hiding out in between cruise tours."

If Ryleigh had been worried before, now her adrenaline shot up a notch. "Can we walk together and find the tiki hut? I'd rather sleep there tonight."

"Ryleigh, we're on an islet that's strung together with others by small sandbars, and these little islands are like a strand of pearls

54

in the ocean. They might all connect, but we don't know where. It's better to wait until dawn and walk with a clear head."

"Okay," she was reluctant and disappointed.

Elliot came to her, and gave her a big hug and wet kiss. "Sit on the tube and I'll go get some grub. I'll stay awake tonight and watch for the rescue boat to come back."

"I don't think I can sleep much either. I mean, out here in the open and all, in nature. " She was awed by the beauty and topography of the surrounding area, and the dense vegetation, and sugar white beaches, but a camping trip, with supplies, clothing, bedding, food, and insect repellant would have been a thrilling enough adventure and experience. Not like this. Left behind by a five-star floating hotel.

Her sister, Caleigh, wouldn't have minded. Oh yes, she had a sister. This was one of the secrets she'd kept from Elliot. Not only was Caleigh her sister, but she was Ryleigh's twin. Identical twin.

"I feel you beaming in the dark. Are you smiling?"

"I was thinking how funny this all will be in a day or two when we're back on the ship. This is a beautiful place, and in other conditions, it would make for a great glamping trip."

"Did you say glamping?"

"Yes, a term my friend and I use for glamorous camping." She needed to tell Elliot soon about her past, but not tonight. Why had she panicked earlier and almost told him?

"Okay. I'm intrigued. What's glamorous camping?"

"Well, for one, tents that are almost like buildings, but lightweight, so we can enjoy the unspoiled beauty of nature without the itchy bites, or the sand in places I didn't know sand could get."

"Next time we get stranded, I'll make sure we get glamping lined up. Hold down the fort; I'll be back in a few."

"Elliot, do you think this came from the cruise ship? Do you think the ship is okay? What if it crashed, or worse, sank?" She didn't really think it would have sunk, but she was beginning to worry about worst case scenarios. Ryleigh felt faint from the coconut creaming. But she let Elliot lead her to the inner tube.

"Hard to tell. It could have been left here from one of the passengers earlier in the day. Sit tight." He walked a few steps toward the brush, looking up at the trees.

"Okay. And I'll take a frozen Pina Colada." She yelled. And then more quietly, she said, "Screw my massage and manicure, I'd rather have my own island for the night. " She said it apprehensively, still not sure of what to feel. Were they going to be picked up in the morning? Why had their rescue guy promptly left? When would they be back? These were questions that mystified her and left her own professional judgments and insights useless. She'd skip the next Zig Ziglar seminar and attend the conference on surviving a cruise ship excursion abandonment.

"That's my girl. Now let me find something to eat. You sit your pretty ass down in this doughnut and curl your sexy legs up over the edges. You don't even need to touch the ground."

She watched as Elliot's silhouette disappeared into the dense brush, and she wondered what would happen if he never came back. She felt in her heart, that for once in her life, she was dependent on another human for survival. Someone she barely knew.

NINETEEN
RAL at Sea

THE ROYAL AHOY cruised silently into the dark night. All scheduled events had been canceled for the evening, but the restaurants were open. Several decks were closed and guarded, and many were roped off with yellow and black striped plastic hazard tape.

Lilah passed the upper deck and glided down the wide, carpeted, open stairwell, without using the brass handrails, taking two steps at a time to get to the infirmary. She wanted to check with the doctor to see how the injured passengers and Captain Peter were doing.

The waves had damaged the pool deck, and rumor had it that several passengers, not in their staterooms, had been washed to sea. Lilah prayed silently that everyone was safe.

"Hi, Theresa, how many patients have checked in?"

"Hi, Lilah." Nurse Theresa reviewed a chart in a manila folder, barely taking her eyes off it to greet Lilah. "I was just completing the paperwork for the fifteenth passenger."

"All from the waves?" Lilah tugged on her hair, still wet under her hat. She, herself, had been stuck in her room, but left as soon as the ship leveled out. Sprays of ocean water had misted her as she ran for the employee lounge. She'd waited there for a few minutes before learning of Captain Peter's injury, and some of the passengers' fates.

"Yes. If I counted the amount of norovirus sickness, we would have over 76 passengers sick in their rooms."

The norovirus sickness had proliferated in the RAL cruise ships, as in the Celebrity and Royal Duchess lines. Norovirus sickness, Montezuma's revenge at sea, had become a major threat in the cruise industry, and all employees had been exposed on a cruise, and many had caught it themselves. Lilah had been laid out for three days on a cruise two years ago. She'd slept on a cot in the employee lounge, and thankfully Trevor had been on that cruise and kept her company, aiding her as she fought the terrible cruise sickness.

"Did you see the waves? They were such freak waves that smashed into the ship and flooded passengers' cabins, broke restaurant windows, and sent all these terrified travelers screaming for the doctors," Theresa said as she flexed her fingers.

"Oh my. I was in my cabin when I heard the wall of water hit the ship. It's crazy. Thank God more weren't hurt." Lilah watched Theresa curl and uncurl her fingers.

"Doctor said the vessel was struck by three abnormally high waves more than 38 feet high. They even broke glass windshields in the forward section. Peter was hurt, two people known have died, and fourteen are presumed dead..." Theresa was speaking while still preoccupied with the charts in her hands.

"Dead? Oh my God. Are they sure? That's major."

"Several people saw a few passengers washed overboard, and a lady broke her ankle racing on board after the island excursion, plus several head injuries with concussions." She stopped and, with an expressionless, unsmiling face, Theresa added, "I suppose you want to know about the Captain."

Lilah felt a flush burn on her cheeks, and she looked down at her shuffling feet. "How is he?"

"He's resting. Big gash on his face where he must have hit the throttle or had broken glass thrown at him. John was out of the control room when it happened. He just found him there, unconscious."

"Oh my. Can I—"

"Yes, Lilah, go ahead. He asked about you."

Lilah gave Nurse Theresa's hand a squeeze and hustled down the hall toward the infirmary rooms.

"He's in zero five." She heard Theresa yell after her.

Before entering room E405, she tapped lightly on the door.

"Open." A strong voice hollered.

When she entered the room, Peter was cradling a cell phone to his ear, and studying a large rolled-out map on the table swung over his midsection, the paper spilling onto the bed. When he spotted her, his expression went from a tight jaw to a smile of relief that spread across his face. She noticed a large white bandage wrapped under his left chin and up to his ear.

"That's right, officer. Hey, look forward to meeting you, too. I gotta run. Will do." He clicked off his phone and tossed it over the map.

"Come here." He patted the bed to his right. "Thank God you're okay."

"Hi, Peter." She moved into the room slowly.

"Throw that stuff on the chair." He winked, making her feel uncomfortable, even though she had dated Peter in the past. But now Trevor was courting her. Trevor was always there for her.

"How are you?" She asked shyly.

"Don't worry about me. I've seen a lot worse." He touched the bandage. "I'm relieved that you're fine."

"I'm okay physically, but you look like you've been in a fight."

"You can say that. This ship, she can do that to her captains sometimes, especially when Mother Nature surprises her."

"And others?"

"We lost some, Lil." His eyebrows gathered in with a pained expression.

Lilah sat on the edge of the map, squashing it, feeling heat behind her eyelids as the tears built up. "Oh no." So it was true what Theresa had told her. She hurt inside, sympathizing over the dead passengers.

The Captain placed his arm around her and rubbed her shoulders, comforting her.

"It's crazy. I was just on the phone with the local government and the U.S. Coast Guard. They're continually looking for survivors. They recovered three bodies. They may fly a helicopter out as far as the excursion island, if all the missing aren't recovered, even though we were long gone from that area."

"No. This has never happened." Lilah took a deep, pained breath and opened and closed her eyes, imagining the scared passengers as they'd been thrown to sea. *Did they die instantaneously? Did they drown slowly? Scream for help? Did I know them? Oh God.*

"Never happened on my watch, and I've been a captain for fifteen years now. Terrible news. Just terrible." He pulled Lilah away, looking deep into her eyes and whispered, "Sorry we missed dinner. We'll have some time off and maybe we can meet then."

"Sure. But I can't even think about that right now. I am scheduled to go to Portugal to see family. What will happen for the next cruise?"

"Not sure when another cruise will take place. There's a lot to do. We're not even sure how many are missing. The work will be done by authorities, not this crew. There'll be interviews, and press conferences, and ironically, the sale went through on the take-over yesterday."

She had heard some of the executives call it a "take-over" versus a merger of the cruise lines, bitter about new management. "Will this ship be used again?"

"Sure, over time, but not now. Different routes are planned. Different islands. Different crews and staff." He shook his head.

60

"We'll still work together?" She wondered if this would be the last time she'd see Peter, just when they were starting their renewed friendship. They had been lovers on their cruises several years ago, but it had ended abruptly. Lilah had heard rumors he was back with his wife. But this cruise was different; he'd spent more time with her.

He leaned against her and only then did she realize he was wearing a thin gown under the blankets. She inched away from him. She'd lost her train of thought.

"Lil, I'll plan on it. You know I can influence the crew that I select for the cruises. You've done a great job. And — "

The door opened slightly and then stopped. "Sorry, man, didn't know you had company." John's voice rang through the cracked door.

Lilah jumped off the bed, relieved at the intrusion.

"John, come in. You remember Lilah? Well, of course you do. Must be the gash in my head," Peter said, laughing it off.

"John," Lilah nodded.

"Hey, Lil. How are the passengers on decks 6 & 7?" John asked straight out. If he was embarrassed or surprised to find her there, he didn't show it in the least bit.

"I'm on my way now to check in.

Peter, I've got to get back. Anything I can do for you?" She fluffed the area where the map sat crumpled on his bed.

"No. Thank you, Lil. I promise to make sure we get that next job soon." When John turned away from the bed, Peter held his fingers to his ear and mouthed, "I'll call you." He smiled a familiar grin as she nodded, and then slipped out the door.

Lilah, once out in the hallway, slumped the weight of her back against room five's door. Still shaking her head in disbelief, she couldn't bring herself to leave. She held her hand to her mouth and, right before she could move her feet, she heard John say to

Peter, "Claudine reported that the three dead passengers suffered fatal injuries from the glass shards and ripped-out window frames and furniture. So far, they have recovered four bodies, and it looks to be eight passengers missing."

TWENTY
Day Two

BACK ON THE island, it was nearly daylight, but Elliot had not slept. Not even a doze.

He walked the horizon, guarding the spot where Ryleigh slept. He checked all the crushed coral passages, several times, to the forest. He checked each scratch of the branches, each screech of a bird. He had tried watching the water, but it was too dark in the sliver of the moonlight. There were no lights. Tomorrow night, he would make a fire.

He wondered, would there still be a tomorrow night here? What had gone so wrong on the cruise ship that they could miscount the passengers? *Why isn't the Coast Guard here? Or the Navy? Or search and rescue helicopters? Why is the rescue tube off the ship?*

He memorized all their surroundings just like he was trained to do. He knew the shadows of the coconut palms, the sound the waves made as they slapped the shoreline and the animal noises, and everything was in the right place.

Ryleigh had slept restlessly after their frugal dinner of coconut meat and milk, breadfruit and berries. She had been a trooper, and he knew she would in the short run, but what if they were there longer than one night? He drank a small dribble of coconut juice out of a half coconut.

He had forgotten how hard it was to get the outer husk off, for the warm milk inside. He'd been amused at how Ryleigh had licked a thin trickle of the coconut milk, her tongue greedily grabbing for the sweet nectar as its warm milk soaked her chin.

She had squealed and said the milk was "warm, wet and sweet," and that "it was the most delicious thing she had ever tasted!"

Elliot had been waking her and checking her pupils and responses to his questions.

Had she been trying to tell him something earlier?

He paced the strip of beach along the shoreline in the early dawn light. He had memorized his and Ryleigh's footprints, noting the shell and bird claw patterns in the sand. With the new day, he knew he could sit down and rest, with one eye open.

Ryleigh was up before he could catch a few minutes of rest. Her eyes were glowing, warm and loving as she stretched.

He bent and kissed her shoulder. "Good morning. How are you feeling? I was up late and just barely fell asleep." From the sun's position, he gauged it to be about 6:45.

"My head hurts, but I'm ready to go to the hut and catch the next ferry back to the cruise ship," she said, gently nibbling on her lower lip.

Elliot stood up and wrapped his arms around her, and their lips connected. They kissed with parted mouths for seconds. He was so hungry for her, but knew she wouldn't want to make love before going to the hut.

"You're so beautiful. You slept on a sandy beach in your bikini and you look gorgeous as ever." He noticed a line of red bumps on her white skin, running the length of her waist just above her bikini line, and he figured sand chiggers had burrowed under her skin, making their food tunnels.

As if she knew what he was thinking, she began scratching the red marks. "Thanks, Elliot. I feel achy all over, but rested. I'm so happy to be with you. I'm ready to go whenever you are."

She stretched her arms overhead and twisted to each side, wincing with a grimace with each turn.

64

"Do you want anything else to drink before we get going?"

"Venti, Café latte chai, no whip."

"I think I saw a Starbucks along the way. Do you want any more coconut water? I saved a few swallows."

He handed her a coconut and she drank from it.

"Save some for me." Elliot smiled. He knew he'd be fine, and in fact they both could last 4 to 6 days without any water, but he knew that wasn't likely to happen.

"You can get some on the ferry or at the hut."

It amazed Elliot how confident Ryleigh was that there would be a ferry waiting at the tiki hut side of Keg Key. He didn't know why not, but something inside him said that if they were waiting at the hut, there would have been spotlights and people searching and calling, and boats around the island. He had seen absolutely nothing all night – barely a fish hopping out of the water.

"Of course I can." He felt guilty as soon as he said the words. "Grab the tube. I have a feeling we may need it."

"Why?"

"We have to cross a channel. You can float and I'll pull you.
"

"Good idea, because there's no way these muscles can swim again. I'm so sore from all the swimming yesterday." She propped the inner tube sideways and straddled it.

"We'll see. I'll drag it in the sand. Let me go piss–"he stopped and corrected himself. "Let me go the bathroom and then we'll get started."

He was pleased to see Ryleigh looking somewhat rested, and smiling as she balanced on the inner tube. With his back to Ryleigh, he kept talking. "At least the storm is gone. It's a great day for a walk on the beach. If there's any left, bring the breadfruit; it could take hours, the way I have the route laid out. It weaves us around the point and a wide jetty, but it keeps us from going the mountainous way. We have the sun to guide our direction, unlike the dense clouds of yesterday."

Elliot kissed the top of Ryleigh's warm forehead. "Are you ready?"

She smiled at him hopefully.

TWENTY-ONE

RYLEIGH AND ELLIOT walked briskly along the seashore. The sand was firm and packed, like a concrete sidewalk, the closer they were to the water. They chose hugging the water's edge over the mushier sand further up the beach, which had felt like powdery quicksand grabbing at their feet.

Ryleigh's blistered and sore feet thudded in the sand as she moseyed close behind Elliot, trying to orient herself on where they were on the connecting islands. She was covered with sand and dirt smudges, and her hair had escaped its elastic tie. She knew she must look ridiculous, but frankly she was too tired to care. She had never covered so much distance on foot and by sea in her life. Swimming and jogging were not her athletic choices.

She hated the feeling of being lost, missing the ferries and being not in control. She had been losing control of her life for the past few months. She felt her life was not anchored, or had had no roots since her parents' death, when structure had broken to pieces, and her sister had run away. Even at work, she had purpose, but now she didn't and was fighting against time, weeks before the class action lawsuit. The threats against her life were more immediate, and viable; she wasn't imagining being trailed and watched. This cruise had been an escape and had saved her sanity.

Ryleigh wanted to tell Elliot about the dangers she had left behind at home, but was afraid he'd become upset. What had he thought about last night? Her dehydrated ramblings?

They walked for an hour in silence while her stomach rumbled and her legs went to rubber.

Elliott stopped and offered her breadfruit. She shook her head. "My intestines will punish me if I send any more breadfruit down them."

Elliott took a few bites and stuck the fruit in his shorts.

67

"You never talk about your family." Ryleigh walked closer to Elliot, avoiding the rubber tube he dragged behind him.

"Not a lot to share. My mother died when I was very young. My dad remarried. My brother and I called her 'Mother Finn.'"

"M.F. Uh oh. Is that good or bad? Did you like her?"

"Mother?" Elliot looked at her for a minute. "Yes, praised me and Ron constantly. My dad was happy with her. He was a good provider, a loving dad and husband, a perfect athlete in his day, and he rose steadily in the ranks at the police station, until a few years ago when he retired, and he's now a private investigator."

Ryleigh loved that Elliot was opening up to her. This was the most he'd ever talked to her about his family. The getaway had the makings of bringing them closer. Maybe now was a good time for some truths from herself. She would try another approach.

Elliot stopped and placed the float's frayed rope in his other hand.

"Do you want me to pull the tube for a while?" She noticed it had left red marks on his fingers.

"No. I'm good."

They stopped and watched a few dolphins frolic in the water. She welcomed the breather, and rested before they continued their walk.

She grabbed his hand and they walked along like two lovers out for a vacation stroll, not like a couple looking to be rescued. "What would you do..." she didn't have a clue how to ask him the question.

"About what?" He interrupted her thought.

"Well, if you were a guy and found out something about a girl you were dating wasn't true, or that she had lied?"

"What are you saying? Have you been lying to me?"

68

"I was just talking hypothetically, like in this movie I saw." Ryleigh had no idea where she was going with this. She needed to stop lying about her life and tell someone she trusted.

"Well, I guess it depends on the lie. I mean, sometimes people hold secrets because they're protecting someone they love."

"Exactly. But in the end, don't you think the person they're protecting may want to know the truth?"

Elliot let go of her hand and ran his hand through his hair, his muscles shining under the early dawn light.

Boy, does he look sexy.

"What's this all about, Ryleigh? A movie? Or you trying to ask me something?" he asked in a loud voice, to be heard above the waves.

That was a switch. Why would Elliot feel this was about him? Hmmm. *Who is this guy I'm falling in love with? What secrets could he have?*

"I was just talking about a movie. Let's drop it." *For now,* she thought.

Ryleigh could tell Elliot was trying to keep her mind off the long walk on the windy beach, and keep her hopes off what they may find back at the excursion camp. He kept pointing out birds, cloud patterns and other random points-of-interest.

"Ry, tell me a good beach walking story about you, not some movie. Tell me about your life growing up, or about college or how you ended up at Dexco Pharmaceuticals."

She tried to think of the last time, including her mom, someone had called her Ry. She liked the sound of it.

"I have an MBA from Tulane, Magna Cum Laude."

"Seriously?"

"Dead serious."

"I have a 'finally-cum-laude' from Florida, if that counts."

"Ha ha. I doubt that."

69

"No seriously, I was a freshman… for three years."

Ryleigh laughed. She loved how he could so easily take her mind off of her troubles. He always did that to her.

"My parents were amazing people," she continued, a blurry shadow passing over her eyes when she mentioned her family. "They were incredibly smart, family dedicated, hard-working parents. Because of their travel agency, we traveled a lot. They took me with them whenever they could."

"That's where you get your world views."

"Yes." He knew most of her background from their dates.

"Share more. I'm not going anywhere."

"I guess we have talked, but not about everything." She felt a guilty knot when she said, 'not everything.'

"So tell me everything about Ryleigh Lane. So what happened? Were your parents disappointed when you didn't take over the family agency?"

"No. They knew the internet was changing that business tremendously. Besides, they wanted me to follow my dreams."

"Dexco was your dream?"

"No, pharmaceuticals were. I wanted to make a difference to people they helped. Working for Dexco made me feel I was making a small contribution. It didn't always feel like the perfect fit, but close enough." What else could she tell him? She had, at first, liked her work and her life, and her small circle of friends. But today that was all gone. She paused to look out over the vast sea.

"In Chicago, it's so different."

"What do you mean? The ocean versus the lake?"

She laughed. "That, too. It is beautiful here. I could look at the sea every day and never get tired of it, but I was referring to the business world. I thought eventually I'd get used to the closet-sized offices filled with professional suits and wingtip shoes, my overloaded lab desk, and a crowded calendar."

"But you aren't?"

She shrugged. "I felt so pressured to get that first job out of school. I wish I'd had more choices. I thought I'd adapt to the company culture. I just haven't." She held back from telling him so much.

"Here's the thing. It's a little scary entering the business world. You go from sleeping in all morning if you skip class, to working non-stop, long hours."

"You skipped classes?"

"I'm just saying. I wasn't perfect."

She pointed toward a pelican diving for his dinner. "I just love watching them. They look like prehistoric birds with their massive beaks and food pouches." When she stopped to look out at the sea, she smelled water and fish, and she wished to God she'd thought to grab some snacks yesterday to take on their romantic love hike.

"You're avoiding the part about telling me everything about you."

"What else is there to know?"

"I know you've told me before, but do you want to talk about their deaths?"

"No. Not really. Not now. What about you, Elliot? Tell me something that no one knows about you?"

"Me, hmm. That would be a lot. I'm not big on sharing."

"So I've noticed. I have known you for almost a year and we've been on two dozen dates, and yet I feel like I barely know you."

"What's there to know?"

"Tell me something about you that hardly anyone knows, and nothing about you being a history teacher."

"Okay. I wore glasses when I was two years old to correct a lazy eye."

"I bet you were cute."

"What do you mean, 'were cute'?" He turned around and chased her off the path a little. He pulled her to him, forcefully but in a gentle way, and planted a warm kiss on her lips. When she pulled away, he had crossed his eyes at her. She laughed at his silly face.

"Hey, look. We're at the bend. Finally!" She took off in a run to the end of the strip of beach.

"I see it! There's the tiki hut!"

Elliot let go of the tube and raced to where the beach ended at the black rocks. There, across a few hundred meters of sea, was another leg of Keg Key, and at the ankle sat the small tiki hut of the Royal Ahoy cruise line.

Ryleigh watched as Elliot shaded his eyes to look out at the point. There were no rescue boats or any signs of life.

"Elliot, where are the boats? And the people?" She felt her flushed face turned ashen as the color ran out of it, and her knees weakened. The knot on her head throbbed.

"We may have been forgotten." The words spilled out of him.

She couldn't stand it anymore. It wasn't fatigue, hunger – or thirst. It was the empty island, dead calm and quiet, straight in front of them, the end of their journey. For the first time in Ryleigh's life, she fainted.

TWENTY-TWO
Brush Island Creek

"STAY ALERT, Ryleigh." Elliot was guiding the inner tube that she floated on, through the passageway that would get them to the tiki hut.

"I still can't believe we were left behind."

Elliot had discussed it with her at least three times already. Once she had recovered from the fatigue, he had convinced her to make the final part of their journey through the water to the tiki hut. They were crossing the center of the barbell, a river, a still and strangely green flowing stream of brackish water. The sides of the water banks were all tangled with vines and bramble.

"Something must have happened during the storm that made the cruise ship depart the area. They'll be back. I promise." Elliot knew they would be looking for them soon. If anything, his team would eventually miss him – not his brother, but yes, the team. The team he couldn't tell Ryleigh about.

"How many days did you say you took off work? Won't your boss be looking for you? "Ryleigh wiggled in the tube.

"It's still only day 4 of our cruise. No one will be missing me for at least two weeks." Maybe longer. He knew in his line of work that he could disappear for months and no one thought anything about it. That's why he didn't like to get involved with anyone. But Ryleigh was different. Despite her girly exterior, she was tough inside. He wanted to tell her his secrets, and end the lying, but not yet.

"What about you, Ryleigh? When are you due back to work?"

"A few weeks," she said softly. "Don't you think the cruise ship will realize we never checked in?"

"I'm sure they will send someone soon." He guided the tube over a large rippled wave.

As the sun bore down on them, high and hot, a cooler dense air began to flow up from the water they were crossing. The inner tube was a safe harbor for Ryleigh. Elliot guided it, encountering little resistance from the water currents as it gathered speed – at first just a faint stirring, then a noticeable current, becoming a downhill push through the inlet, spreading the algae and sea grass open as they pushed through.

"Are there snakes in here?"

"Maybe, and possibly barracudas or crocs." Elliot didn't want to alarm her again. He didn't want another fainting episode, but he had to make her aware of what they were traveling through.

"Are you bullshitting?" Ryleigh cringed.

"I'm serious. Saltwater crocodiles enjoy catching a wave and can travel hundreds of miles, kind of like surfing on the ocean currents. So there have been species to be known to move between oceanic islands."

"Just great. That's not the answer I was looking for. My half naked ass is sticking out through this inner tube, waiting for a croc or a snake to take a nip of it."

"When we get settled at the hut, I'll be the one taking nips of your ass."

"Hmm, I look forward to that, but for now, let's make sure there are no creatures that beat you to it. And, crocs in saltwater?"

"There are saltwater crocs that have been known to swim over six hundred miles."

"Geez, Elliot, I would never have dreamed that forty-eight hours ago, while I was sunning myself at the main deck pool, that I now would be stranded and floating though a stream filled with deadly, monstrous creatures. I'm thirty-two years old, never married, had a great career, and still want kids someday. One minute I'm worried about a massage, the next I'm praying the cooks left some food behind in the tiki hut."

Elliot let her ramble on for several minutes, preoccupied with their predicament, and maneuvered past a large shaded area under the water. *God, please don't let it be a shark, or even so much as a stingray.*

"Did you see that?"

"What?" he lied.

"That dark movement below us. Ewe!" She used her hands to pull her butt and both legs to a kneeling position on the tube. "Come on, Elliot, jump on with me!" the sound of panic seeped out of her voice.

"It's okay. I'll paddle slowly, not stirring the bottom. We're almost there." Sandy mud oozed between his toes and eventually buried his ankles as he squished in soupy muck and algae-filled water to his waist. But he had no plans to float above it on the tube with Ryleigh.

The afternoon heat began to swell their bodies, puffing out their fingers and toes like sausage links, as they continued through the bog. *Don't panic. It's the first rule of survival. Remain calm.* He always did.

TWENTY-THREE

WHEN RYLEIGH crawled over the rocks jetting out into the sea and landed on the smooth beach, the hut was there.

"Elliot, there! We're close!"

She hurried her pace and Elliot had to jog to keep up with her. "Slow down, Ryleigh, we'll be there in minutes."

"It is beautiful." She slowed to a fast walk.

"There's not a lot of rivers and natural water run-off on the island, so the waters around it stay clear. The corals surrounding it add to the beauty."

"Why do you know so much about it?"

"I studied it before I chose this cruise line."

"So how did we get so lost? Surely, one bad swim couldn't have ended with us so turned around."

"I guess the blustery storm and erratic ocean swells threw me off."

"Well, we're back, and it looks like the hut is still in place. Maybe there's a radio inside. And we can use my cell to call for help. We will be back on the boat in time for lunch." Ryleigh didn't push Elliot on the mess-up any further. It was both their faults for their unfortunate situation. She was a bundle of stress, and she feared speaking, anxious that he'd hear it in her voice.

The excursion beach where the tiki hut sat now looked abandoned. Empty spots where the ferry boats were once moored, sand castles washed away... crowded colorful towels and the noisy beach goers that occupied them, long gone. There were white and yellow plastic lounge chairs stacked in scattered rows near the hut, the volleyball net sagged in the middle with shredded palm throngs weaved in it, and the long stone bar-b-q pit, now covered with sand, looked ancient. Coconuts were scattered everywhere.

"Wow. It looks like a bomb went off here."

The tiki hut sat on stilts, and the walls and roof were made of thick palm branches resembling bamboo. The door was a sheet of rustic metal, and two windows were covered with burlap tied in place with grisly rope.

Without another word, they both jogged to the front door of the tiki hut. It was locked.

"Now what? I'm dying of thirst. Do you think there's drinks in there?"

Elliot walked around the hut and Ryleigh followed him. On the left side, she saw a black strap sticking out of the sand. "Elliot, what's this?"

He knelt in the sand and pulled out a duffle bag. He peered inside first, then rummaged through it.

"Is there a cell phone? A radio?"

"No, but there is this." He dumped the contents on the sand while pulling out a large knife. "If I can't break the lock, I'll cut the thatched sides to get in."

Ryleigh looked at the knife in Elliot's hands. He looked very comfortable holding it. The other items on the sand looked like a collection of men's clothing, men's toiletries, a girly magazine, and a small red iPod.

"What's this? A radio?"

"No, that's an older iPod. Music only."

Ryleigh tossed it onto the clothes and followed Elliot to the front of the hut.

"Well, cut the palms off. I'm dying to see what's inside."

"Let me see what I can do without destroying the hut."

"Okay, hurry."

While Elliot worked on the door, Ryleigh looked around. The place looked to have been abandoned in a hurry. But there were still two port-a-potties lined up near the brush, stacks of chairs and umbrellas, and a cage that held sports equipment. "Look Elliot, his and hers potties."

He grinned, but kept on working.

The lounge chairs had been stacked off the beach, so at first glance, Ryleigh had no idea where her cell phone could be.

The hut overlooked the shallow part of the beach and was on the end of a small pier that looked, at one time, to have been used for boats to tie up to. Now the water around it was too shallow for boats.

Elliot dug the knife into the lock. After a few minutes, the lock fell to the ground, opening the door as smoothly as if he'd held the key.

"Wow, I'm impressed. Did you use to be a burglar?"

He winked at her. "After you."

They entered the living room sized hut.

"Water, there." She knelt down on the floor under the shelves and attempted to rip the plastic off the case of bottled water. "Give me the knife."

She stabbed at the plastic wrappings with the knife until she retrieved a bottle. She pulled the cap off and drank it like she was shot-gunning a beer; it tasted like liquid heaven.

"Slow down, Ryleigh. Your body needs to register it."

Elliot picked up a bottle, pried off the top, and slowly wet his lips. Then he dumped it down his throat. Water ran down his bare chest.

Ryleigh took another bottle and did the same thing.

She laughed at the two of them with water dripping off their chins and running down their arms and chests.

Elliot pulled her close and kissed her lips. "You're going to be okay, Ryleigh. "

Ryleigh felt that to be true in her heart. But why had he not said, 'We're going to be okay?'

"Yes, we are, Elliot Finn. Yes, we are. How about lunch? Cheetos? Lays?" She grabbed a few small bags of chips and tossed them at Elliot.

They ripped them open and sat on the floor, eating chips and drinking water. Elliot told her a story about how his mom would use crumbled Cheetos on top of cheese grits. He laughed when he told the story and his eyes sparkled when he talked. She wondered what it would be like to wake up beside him every morning, and spend every meal eating across the table from him.

Elliot grabbed her hands and her palms were damp.

"What do you want to do while we wait to get rescued?" He smiled at her, and it had a mischievous hint about it, as though he had a hidden secret. Something she would never know.

"I want to look for my cell."

Elliot pouted and ran his hand up her leg. "Bring me those delicious lips."

She added, "Look for the cell, only after we break in the hut."

She grabbed his hand and looked at him with her most sultry and lascivious eyes. She untied her swimsuit top.

Elliot grabbed a stack of souvenir t-shirts off the shelf and threw them on the wood-planked floor. They made love, lost in the neon t-shirts for hours.

TWENTY-FOUR
Day Three

RYLEIGH WOKE, stretched, and every muscle screamed in protest. If this morning was painful, another night's sleep in the hut would be no better. But at least it wasn't on the beach. That first night of sleeping on the beach had been a crash course in hell instigated by one angry, coconut knot on her head. She rolled over the sandy planked floor that was her crude bed.

Elliot was already up and gone.

All night, she'd felt their shoulders touching and his arms embracing her from time-to-time, and crickets screaming in the brush behind the hut. She'd barely slept. She'd kept her ears open for the rescue boat.

Thank God there'd been provisions left behind in the hut. *Won't they be coming back for us?*

They had eaten four mini bags of stale Cheetos and drunk four bottles of water. She stared up at the shelves of items, some useless and some useful. Rows and rows of suntan lotion and bug spray. Hallelujah! Very useful. Colorful, hot pink, blue, yellow, and red plastic sand pails and shovels, and sand molds, stacked another row of shelves. Not so useful. These were similar to the beach toys she'd used when she was a child playing at the shores of Lake Michigan. A few straw hats and sunglasses, mostly children's sizes, and snorkels, fins, several sundry kits, souvenirs, and cruise ship themed pieces of sportswear, and a limited variety of groceries and snacks. An odd sight was a small stack of toothbrush kits. She had a hard time imagining even the most hygiene-focused beach-goer wanting to brush their teeth with bottled water or ocean water. But hey, she wasn't complaining, and running a dry brush over her teeth right now sounded refreshing.

80

The hut had no alcohol or fresh food that she could see.

She rolled off the bed, cursing her sore body and vowing to get in shape once she returned to Chicago. Just in case she needed to swim after a ferry boat during a tropical storm.

"Once I return. When will that be?"

"Talking to yourself," Elliot said from behind her. She relaxed and leaned into him as he came near, feeling the strength of his arms and torso.

"Yes. I was asking the ocean gods, where the hell is our rescue boat?"

"Ryleigh, we can't do much about that right now. So let's make a plan while we can. Think of the great story we'll have to tell when we're back on the ship."

She knew they both didn't want a story. She was hiding from someone, something, and she promised herself she would tell him soon. *But when?*

For the first time since they'd met, she felt a special bond suggesting that she could trust him. If she told him, would that put Elliot in danger, too? Could she risk it?

They stood in uncomfortable silence for a few seconds.

"Just look at all this stuff. Is this considered breaking and entering?" She had watched last night while Elliot hacked the lock off the flimsy hut door. He'd made burglary look like child's play.

"Under the circumstances, I'd say, no." His mouth quirked up, amused. "Come on, while you were sleeping, I made something for breakfast." His voice was excited with adventure.

"Not Cheetos again." She wrinkled up her nose at him as he led her away from the hut.

"No, I was thinking eggs."

"Eggs? There's a refrigerator?"

"No, unfortunately not. Before you woke up, I managed to snag a few edible small eggs, and mixed them with water and coconut milk."

"Yuk, Elliot. What kind of birds? Pigeons? Seagulls?"

"No, a much larger bird."

She looked up in the sky. "Will the mother bird be attacking us?"

"No. I'm sorry for her loss, but we have plans to eat her and her mate for lunch or dinner."

"Elliot, how did you do that?" He continued to surprise her. How did he know how to snare a bird? Just like with the berries and fruit, he knew which ones were edible.

"I'll show you later. Not a big deal. Come, you need to eat."

She was ravenous, but skeptical. Such a mysterious man she was stranded with. She'd always felt he was sexy, fun and adventurous, but this wilderness side was a pleasant surprise. Making Huckleberry Elliot Finn even hotter.

"Come, let's eat. It could be days before I can get more."

Ryleigh caught the word *days,* and a small gasp of surprise popped from her. *What does he know, anyway?*

"You still feel it could be days before we're rescued?" Seriously, she was about to eat a pigeon or some other wild bird's egg, probably the size of a quarter. She should have been eating filet mignon and eggs benedict, and Belgium waffles with warm maple syrup.

"I was thinking last night that maybe something did happen with the cruise ship that has kept the authorities occupied," he said as he guided her over to the excursion island's large outdoor grill and fire pit.

"Really?"

"Who knows, but anything is possible. Sit here." He brushed off the lawn chair and steered her gently into its strappy seat of faded yellow plastic webbing.

He ran for an umbrella and planted it over her chair, such that the shade covered her whole body. She sat silently, watching him tend to the coconut shell mixture of gooey eggs from the large, dead island bird.

She suppressed a gag in her throat and was surprised that her stomach responded with a hunger growl. *Try not to think of the source of breakfast. Think about this sexy half-naked man, cooking wild game eggs, on a deserted tropical island.*

Elliot poured the coconut shell egg mixture onto a tin baking tray resting on the grill. Immediately, the sizzling smells of the scrambled mixture reached her and her saliva glands almost exploded with drool. She wasn't thinking of the dead tropical bird; she was only focused on her only morsel of food, besides Cheetos, since a few days ago.

"Where'd you get oil?"

"Left underneath the propane tank." He gestured toward the cabinet under the grill housing.

Her spirits rose as he presented to her a scrambled dark yellow mixture of egg yolks and white coconut chunks, centered amidst colorful tropical flowers.

"Wait. Final touch." Elliot crushed a few Cheetos and sprinkled them on top of the mixture.

"Cheetos again?"

"My mama's touch. Besides, wild birds' eggs have a strong flavor, and the cheese will help."

"And the green flakes?"

"Nettle leaves."

"Huh?"

"Sort of an herb."

"Utensils?"

"No. Not yet."

Ryleigh frowned, but didn't hesitate to dig her fingers into the mushy, mustard yellow egg mixture, shoveling it into her mouth.

"Oh my. Oh, yum!" she said between bites and shoving another finger-full into her mouth, feeling a milky film on her lips. "Your turn," she handed the tin platter to Elliott.

He scooped up a few fingers full and ate. "Mmmm." He looked pleased.

"Wow, Elliot, how did you know what to make? How did you find the nest? Are there more eggs?"

"I've been known to cook. You've never had an opportunity to experience waking up at my place."

He was right. They usually met in cities, stayed in hotels, and ate in restaurants.

"These eggs are different, but great. I'd just about eat anything." She picked up the flower and smelled it.

"Don't eat that."

"Aren't some flowers edible?"

"Yes, but not that one. You can eat it, but you might hallucinate."

"Then why is it on the plate?"

"It's important for morale, that every meal we try and make is prepared and presented nicely. It gives us a purpose, helps retain our identities and self-esteem."

"You act like we're here for the long run. I'm sure there's another cruise stopping here in a few days."

He scanned the horizon and then focused his gaze on her.

She nodded toward the ocean. "Any signs of boats, planes, rafts, anything?"

"Afraid not. But I've made a big fire and we'll keep it lit. I'll gather rocks and spell S.O.S. on the beach."

"Okay. Great idea. I'm disappointed I couldn't find my plastic bag with my cell in it. I'm sure it's here, buried somewhere." She scooped another bite of the egg mixture into her mouth.

"The storms have changed the landscape a little, and all the lawn chairs are moved and stacked away. While I'm exploring this morning – why don't you dig?"

"Dig?"

"Yes. Use a pattern like a grid with coordinates and move along the beach, shuffling sand until you come across it."

"Do you really think it's still here? Or did a passenger find it? My clothes, hat, book, everything is gone."

"But your bag could still be buried. And we should look for it."

"Okay, I'll get started after I take a quick, cold, saltwater, shower. I have dried blood, mud, and sand in my hair, and God knows what insects are burrowed under my skin." She physically shivered.

"Okay. I think I saw a few toiletries' in the hut. Use them sparingly. You look great, and it could be days before we're–"

"–there you go again. Acting like it will be days before they come back."

"I'm just saying." His gaze was intense.

"Okay, I'll use sparingly."

Is it really going to be days?

TWENTY-FIVE
Port of RAL

THREE DAYS AGO, fifteen cruise ship passengers were tragically killed or lost at sea, presumed dead, when the Royal Ahoy Cruise Liner, now owned by Celebrity Cruises, was struck and damaged by several large rogue waves.

He read the news article in his file, and then Detective Chandler tossed the file folder on the front seat of his rented abyss blue Kia. He had memorized the flimsy contents.

He lit a cigarette and called his main squeeze, of late.

"Hey, baby. Yep, I made it. Sitting in port now. About ready to talk to crew, passengers, captain – the usual."

Like most cruise line accidents, and as in most of the unfortunate cases he worked, the CEO and Board of Directors for the cruise line usually closed ranks and tried, generally successfully, to suppress the facts of the mishap and deflect the media's attention away from anything that could hurt their cruising industry and their bottom line.

"I should be back in a few days. This is considered a non-event. Large waves. Mother Nature. It's not like the Achilles' Lauro or the Costa Concordia. "Nothing from the other side of the cell phone. He hated when she went silent on him. Her blonde head had too much air space between her shoulders.

"You there? I'm not dealing with hijacking or a pirates attack or drunk captains. This case should be clean-cut," he tried to explain to her.

He was already bored with this girl. She flaked out too much, even for him. He was too used to doing whatever he wanted, when he wanted, without needing to take her plans into consideration. It was time to break up with her and end the relationship.

He was returning to the States the next day, but on a whim, he decided to tell her different. "I'll see you next week when I return."

Chandler exited his vehicle and proceeded to the port where the majestic RAL sat. At the cruise station, he found vacationers staring at names on a blackboard. *Survivors? Or Missing?*

Women looking for their husbands, children for their parents… Chandler stood at the doorway, watching the faces of everyone entering.

He felt something was seriously off. Sure, there were missing people. There was a body that had still not been identified. One chick they'd recovered had an I.D. in her shorts, but it hadn't fit her description.

He had visited the makeshift morgue outside the cruise ship and talked to the local coroner, and of course, being drowned in the salty sea, floating around like fish bait, could disfigure a body. The girl found in the sea looked barely eighteen. The driver's license in her shorts said she was thirty-two. He would book some time with Tammera, the medical examiner who he trusted the most in his world.

He couldn't pinpoint exactly why he felt deep down that something else had gone terribly wrong.

The ship's decks were a blur of activity – insurance men took pictures, security gathered evidence, maintenance crews cleaned up the glass and debris. He recognized in the corner, stacked on an empty table, a few folded-up dark bags – body bags. The last piece of luggage some of these passengers would ever need.

"Detective?" An older man with greyish blonde hair, wearing a white jacket and navy trousers, approached Chandler, scrutinizing him.

Captain Peter, he assumed.

"Hi. You're Captain Peter? Nice to finally meet you. How's the gash? I heard you took some glass shards to the face." Chandler shook Peter's hand.

"I've had worse in barroom brawls. Nothing a few stitches couldn't fix up." The RAL Captain rubbed the bandage, his pale blue eyes distant for a few seconds.

"Going to leave a nasty scar?"

"It won't be my first scar; comes with the job. I'm 20 years Navy."

They spoke quietly so as to not be overheard by the nearby workers.

"Well, if it's any consolation, the scar will be a nice plus for the ladies. Every girl that sees it will ask how you got it and will find out that you're a hero."

"I'm no hero, Mr.–"

"–call me Chandler."

"Okay. Detective Chandler, just doing my job. Now, what questions do you have for me that the FBI, DOT, and RAL management haven't already asked?" The Captain glanced around and then added, "I'd invite you downstairs, but it's quite a mess."

"Were you drinking?" Chandler knew Peter had not been drinking, at least according to the toxicology report from the blood test after he'd checked into the infirmary, but he wanted to see the good Captain's response.

"Not that night, Detective."

Touché.

"Was there an emergency message sent after the first wave?"

"It happened so fast. I have already said all this in my report. Didn't you read it?"

"I did, but it's good to hear from the source."

"No. I didn't radio. I was commanding the ship, and didn't feel immediate danger. After the first wave, the storm seemed to be getting weaker. We telephoned the Coast Guard Station at Castle Cove."

"Steward, John?"

"Yes." Peter rubbed his cheek. His nose twitched, the most prominent feature of his somewhat aristocratic-looking face.

They both watched as several men ran by, one wearing an insignia on his shirt, reading *maintenance crew*.

Peter's eyes followed the guys, then settled back on Chandler.

"I'll need to see the manifest of the cruise ship's log." Chandler said.

"That's not a problem"

"I appreciate you helping. Is there a morgue on board?"

"Yes. It can accommodate five bodies."

"Okay. How'd that evening go? Can you tell me what you remember?"

"We left in a rush. I cruised her through the reefs off Point Fina. I even saw the sun break through a hole in the dark clouds. I remember seeing a gorgeous sunset leading a blaze of orange over the Three Sister Islands. By the time we cruised the middle sister, we'd passed through the deep channel between the two islands. We cruised by the village and there were a few other boats in harbor, starboard." He paused, then continued.

"There were a few sport boats trolling back into the coast. I kept pushing her steadily, straight to the open sea."

"What time was that?" Chandler asked.

"By the time we hit the open sea, it was around 8 p.m."

Chandler nodded at Peter, "Keep going."

"Out on the sea, she made good time, even on those waves. I never saw it coming, even though I was looking at all the monitors. Just on the heels of that wild rainstorm. Then, boom."

"Had you warned everyone to return to their rooms?"

"You know RAL; this one we're on, she's not an American vessel."

"I know that. But did you send out warnings?"

"Yeah, when it went from bad to worse, I did. It's more an instinct, and an art, than it is a science. The RAL management, they wanted the casinos open, and the bars and restaurants full, and the pool deck bands playing and the passengers spending their money all night. Management didn't want signs of security running around, warning and rounding up passengers to get below. But I didn't care; I alerted my crew and they teamed up with security and began getting the passengers back to their rooms."

"Well, you went above and beyond. More lives might have been lost if you hadn't ordered the closures." Chandler looked around at the crowds of people working on the ship. Here he was, among them, blending into the group, and every one of them would be urged to keep quiet.

"Like I said, just doing my job." Captain Peter looked at his watch and stood up. "The next thing I knew, I woke up in the infirmary and dawn had broken." He looked up at the ship. "Some god, somewhere, had taken the weather and rough seas a little in hand – but only for a short time. But that's all it took."

Chandler nodded.

"Do you want to go take a look at the control room? I'm headed that way now," Peter said. "And you may want to speak with my co-captain. Fortunately, he was there minutes after the waves hit the ship and knocked me out."

"Sure. I do."

The two walked toward the control room.

90

"What information are they releasing to the press?" Chandler knew this information, too, but wanted to see what Peter knew.

"They'll give as little as possible. The new owners' CEO's cavalier attitude toward the passengers' safety is reprehensible, because he is always more concerned about the bottom-line. And considering the salary this guy makes, he should worry more about pleasing the passengers."

"Yeah, I've heard all the reasons they can't release the information." Chandler knew there were a lot of standards and procedures set up, but in reality, these varied from cruise line to cruise line, from port to port, from country to country.

Chandler spent twenty minutes in the control room, walking through that night with the Captain. When he felt comfortable with every detail, he wrapped it up and sent the Captain on his way. "Captain, take care of your wound."

"Thanks, Detective."

"One more thing..." Chandler yelled out to the Captain as he turned to go downstairs.

"What now?"

"Do you know where most of your crew will be next?"

"We're all on a two month hiatus, company paid."

Chandler whistled. "Nice. So most of your crew will be at their homes? And not on cruises out to sea somewhere."

"Or on vacations. Who knows?"

"Got it." Chandler nodded at him.

"Good luck," Captain Peter said as he turned and bound down a flight of stairs.

Detective Chandler, a retired veteran deputy from the sheriff's marine division out of Tampa, and a bit of a renegade, wore his borrowed FBI vest, giving him free range anywhere on the ship. He wandered to the top deck, toward the front bow of the gigantic liner, looking out into the port. It felt creepy. Like the scene of the *Titanic*. She wasn't moving, the ship was vacant, and he could almost jump to the safety of the piers. Just the way he liked his cruise ships. In port, empty, no suntan lotion needed.

Before he returned to Tampa, he had a few stops to make for interviews. One with a young, Texan, college-aged girl who claimed her traveling companion had disappeared. The ship manifest was indifferent, not showing a missing college girl.

Detective Chandler had been assigned to dozens of cruise ship mishaps, accidents, suicides, thefts, rapes, missing person's cases, and murders, and these rogue high waves were no different. However, after reading the college-aged girl's report, he had some unanswered questions.

This ain't so clean-cut. A few minutes later, he lit a cigarette and stood outside his rental car looking at the huge cruise ship. Something was not right, and he felt it instinctively.

TWENTY-SIX
Day Four

RYLEIGH CRAWLED on all fours, her knees and palms blistered and chafed from the sand.

She raised up and stared across the beach. It was littered with colorful sand pails. Lain out in a checkerboard fashion. Large piles of sand and holes, two-pail-size deep, covered one half of the beach from the tiki hut. More pails lined the beach closest to the sea.

She was proud of her work. It looked like a scene out of *Holes*, a movie she'd gone to years ago with her neighbor's kids. But she wasn't digging for Kissin Kate Barlow's buried loot: she was digging for her cell phone. She was convinced it was still buried in the sand.

The storm had left Keg Key beaches in shambles, and even many of the lawn chairs had disappeared. But she prayed the plastic bag with her cell phone was still buried.

She had been digging for her cell phone since they'd gotten to the tiki hut camp site two days ago.

Elliot had been gone all morning. She often wondered what he did when he explored. It really didn't matter because he always had food for them, and so far, their water and food had been plentiful. They had discussed a plan for rationing if the ferry boat didn't return by the end of the week, though.

They kept a fire that burned and crackled in the fire pit lit most days, and every night.

So far, there had been no signs of boats or planes near the islands. She knew it was a remote, uninhabited area of the sea, but the cruise line company had found it, so it was just a matter of days before some tourist yachts or fisherman discovered them.

"Now if I can just find my damn phone." She yelled at the sand hole she was digging.

By midday, the sun was searing like a boiler, and Ryleigh had a tiki hut souvenir t-shirt tied around her head to keep the dripping sweat from burning her eyes. Her back was sore from being hunched over for the last day and a half. And no matter how much sunscreen she applied, her shoulders and back felt fried. The same feeling she had every night after she loaded on the bug spray. She still felt like she was being eaten alive by invisible mosquitos. She heard the scurry of rats and small rodents outside the hut at night. Beautiful place during the day, creepy at night.

Ryleigh cast an uneasy glance over her shoulder. It was silly, she knew, to be so jumpy about a wide-open empty beach, but the small movements flickering in the dark brush at the end of the beach for the good part of the morning bothered her. She wondered when Elliot would return from exploring.

Occupied with shadows in the woods, she barely felt the plastic shovel buckle. She dug in the hard sand faster, and this time the shovel handle broke.

"Eureka! What is this?" She yelled.

She threw the remains of the green plastic shovel to the side and continued digging with her hands. Scarcely aware that only four days ago, she'd been stressed out over chipped nail polish.

Then she felt it. Plastic. Strings. A handle. She wiped away the remaining sand and, with trembling fingers, she yanked the plastic bag containing her treasure out of the ground.

"Elliot!" She screamed. "I found it."

She looked around for Elliot, but he was still nowhere in sight, and that's when she saw it, a black movement in the brush now five feet in front of her. Her heart dropped into her stomach, and she was unaware that she was backing up, crawfishing across the beach toward the water, her eyes never leaving the brush.

94

At the same time, she reached into the bag and found her cell phone. She powered it on. Thank God. It still had battery power.

She smiled as the familiar screen saver popped up. She entered her code and hit the first name on her saved list, and waited while the international call went through. "Pick up. Pick up, Caleigh! You have to be home."

She heard Caleigh's friendly voice and tears of joy ran down her face, until she heard, "and wait for the tone. " Beep.

Ryleigh stared at the phone, forgetting what to do.

"Oh my God! Pick up, Caleigh! I need help. I'm…" Ryleigh screamed and yelled, "Get away."

A large black bull the size of a canoe raced at her, horns bent to spear her. She ran toward the water's edge, and yelled "Elliot!" She tossed her phone on the sand and belly-flopped headfirst into the water.

TWENTY-SEVEN

ELLIOT HEARD RYLEIGH scream. He trotted, holding the fish he had speared high as he ran through the mangled brush toward the camp.

What in the world could she be yelling about?

He ran onto the beach. Ryleigh bobbed in the aqua sea, whitecaps racing around her and the top of her head peaking above the water. That was a first. She rarely swam alone. She floated on the inner tube a lot, but didn't go swimming; having seen the sharks had made her a land dweller.

"Ryleigh, what's wrong? Why'd you scream?"

"Elliot, did you see it?"

"What?" He scanned the water and the horizon.

"No, not out there. On the beach, a large black bull." She came bouncing out of the water. "I chased away a giant bull," she said, laughing.

"A bull?" He wondered if she was hallucinating. "You didn't eat the red berries, did you?"

"No, I'm not seeing things. It came after me." She strolled toward him. Her face was bright red, her knees scratched up, and then she dove for something black in the sand.

"Ryleigh, what's that?" He pointed at a sandy phone.

"I found it. I found my cell. I called for help, but that giant animal charged me. I swear, Elliot."

"Your phone. Let me see it."

"Oh no, what if it got wet?" She bent down, and dusted sand off her phone; she handed it to him.

He wondered who she had called. When he touched the phone's tiny screen, a bright orange sunset screen saver popped up. "What's your code?"

"One thousand."

Elliot punched 1–0–0–0 into the phone. "You really should think of a safer password."

"Seriously, now you're worried about that? Here?"

"In the future. I'm just saying." Elliot scrolled over the last number called and saw that it had gone through. It was a 312 area code. Chicago.

"Who did you call?" He wondered why she hadn't tried 911.

"Does it matter? Just call someone now."

"You had one call and it was to Chicago. Why?"

"Just give me my damn phone."

"No. Let me make a few calls. I can have help here by the end of the day." He could if he wanted to. But he couldn't. Not yet.

"Just do it." Ryleigh jumped up and down like she had a fish in her bathing suit bottoms. "Call for help, Elliot. Call now!"

He looked at the phone again and dialed a few numbers. He held a key down and the phone went dead.

"I can't believe it was here all the time. We could have left two days ago. Oh my God, this is so awesome."

"I think we may have a problem." He held the phone out to her.

"What? Why is the screen black?"

"Dead. Water, maybe."

"Oh no. "She grabbed it from his hands and hit the power button a few times. She crumbled to her knees in the hot sand and worked frantically to disassemble and remove the case. "I have a water resistant case. It should be fine. I wasn't in the water. Maybe the battery just died." She gasped, blinking saltwater dripping from her eyelashes.

After she got the case off, she turned it over and took off the back. She took out a piece, blowing on everything. "Maybe it just needs to dry in the sun. It looks fine. Maybe it's out of power."

"We'll work on it. Maybe I can get it working somehow."

"Do you really think so?"

"Maybe. Let's eat lunch. You must be starved. Tell me about this hog." He hugged her. "My Ryleigh chasing a hog." She looked amazing. Her cheeks were flushed and her emerald sea goddess eyes were glowing, her mermaid hair tumbling down her back.

"It was a wild hog. Right?"

"I see the tracks here. Looks like a feral boar. It trails back in the brush. He probably saw you rooting in the sand. Not sure why he came out of the brush, but I'm going to hunt it."

"Elliot, you seem more ecstatic about the wild boar than my cell phone."

"I miss meat. What can I say?" What could he say? That he'd never really expected her to find her phone, let alone be able to make a call.

"Meat? Well, get my cell to work and we can call the cruise ship. They can send a seaplane or helicopter and take us back to land. We can have the best steak dinner ever. In a restaurant. Not like this." She turned and stomped her way through the sand. She picked up the plastic bag, looked inside, and laughed. She pulled out her credit card. "Just perfect."

She threw the blue plastic bankcard in the sand and went toward the tiki hut.

Elliot turned around and walked to the trail's edge, studying the hog's tracks. He knew he should do the guy thing and follow Ryleigh, but he couldn't right now.

"Where are you going?" She yelled from the hut's door, straddling the threshold.

"To get us some meat."

"Good luck with that." She turned and slammed the tiki hut door so hard that a few palms fell off.

ISLAND OF LIES

TWENTY-EIGHT

RYLEIGH LAID ON the hard floor of split bamboo secured tightly together with strips of bark, a crisp, new cruise ship t-shirt rolled up as a pillow. She stared at the ceiling, now secured with overlapping fronds, netting, and some metal from the man's port-a-potty. Her very own Huckleberry had added this lining to give them extra protection against the rain and heat. He'd done that their very first day at the hut, leaving one totally intact port-a-potty just for her.

She looked closely at the initials Elliot had carved in the main beam. E.L.F and R.A.L. He had drawn a heart around their initials. Elliot Lee Finn, still a mystery to her. A single force of nature had brought them together, but had it not been for the hurricane, would they eventually have been living together?

As hard as she tried to think of a good lie to tell Elliot about the one phone call she had made, she couldn't. She would just tell him it was to her good friend. Or maybe now was the time to tell him about her sister.

Maybe it was time for some truths.

Shouldn't she tell him about her job? And Dexco executives? And the trial coming up? And why lie about her sister? Once he got the phone to work, he would know who she'd called. *If* they got her cell to work.

She had thought about these things for hours. Elliot still hadn't returned. Maybe she should explore the brush herself and see if she could find him. She unfolded a neon green t-shirt, and struggled to pull it over her head.

Securing the hut door, she stepped off the pier pilings.
Hot and a bit humid, but not brutal today, she thought. A light breeze blew the world clear again. The sunshine, sparkling surf and snow

white sand eased some of the stranded anxiety she'd been feeling. Taking her frustrations out on Elliot was so unlike her. She would make it up to him.

She stared out to the sea and back to the beach. Every time she looked up the beach, she expected to see a couple strolling along hand-in-hand. It just seemed so natural, like in every vacation travel brochure her parents had left around their house. *Come visit the islands! Your dream island vacation awaits you. From Keg Key with love.*

Her postcard would read, *turn memorable, to unforgettable.* Would her postcard show a strolling couple? Some people were made for coupling, for lifelong companionship. Was she? Maybe a year ago, she would have felt that. But lately her life was beginning to become a mess. Sometimes she felt that her stranded life here would be good enough for her, whether or not she ever went home. What did that say about her?

She just wanted to escape the horrible discovery and truths waiting for her back home. She just wanted to escape that world, and to return back to a normal one.

Right now, she needed to find her Huck Finn, and stop worrying about life back home. She needed to find him and apologize for her outburst, and until she did, no amount of ocean breezes would blow her present world clear again.

The brush was thick with trees and shrubs and bursts of colorful blooms. It was always surprisingly quiet. She missed humans. She missed seeing kids at play, and those lovers walking hand-in-hand up the beach, old people walking slowly across a street. The only beings whose paths she crossed, or that had crossed hers, were lizards and snakes, and in that one case, a hog. Elliot had been ecstatic when she'd told him she had seen a wild boar, even more than finding her phone. "Because he missed meat." It just didn't add up.

She continued her walk. How could she have lied about such trivial things? Would Elliot think she was shallow because she would lie about her family and her job? Most women lied about their age, right?

And what about Elliot? He was too smart about island life. Too adventurous. Too content with their situation.

She felt spider webs on every branch, and the tingling feeling they left on her skin. She rubbed her hands over her arms, as she swore she felt a spider on her. Her tangled hair, matted from the rest in the hut, stuck to her back.

She wandered farther into the island. Here there were no answers. There were trees. And shrubs. Mangroves. Ferns. Vines. Snakes. Lizards.

She didn't care. She kicked at the grass as she walked deeper into it and a small black snake slithered under the brambly brush. This wasn't an island; it was a forest. She looked up at the canopy of trees overhead and the baby blue peeking through. There were tall palm trees and short palms, wide-leafed ferns and ferns with small, intricate variegated leaves, and thick vines and thin vines. Vines everywhere. It was like the Garden of Eden where Adam and Eve met, and where the snake lured them and they ate the forbidden fruit. But unlike Adam and Eve, they wouldn't be getting kicked out of paradise anytime soon, it seemed. It was an island of lies.

She heard grunting sounds coming from the trail to the left. She went a few feet down the trail. She could see Elliot bent over the hog, using a large knife on it.

Elliot standing over the boar looked like a choreographed horror movie. He sliced the 6-inch blade through the boar's body, laying it flat on the path like a boar-skin rug. She watched silently as a jet of blood shot from the boar's mouth – ssssffft! His knife

102

sliced off the head. With several nerves still firing, Ryleigh saw the headless boar's tail twitch.

Ryleigh, feeling like an outsider, took a step back toward the trail opening. She was used to being left in the dark lately about Elliot and his exploring, so why would hunting be any different, but sneaking up on him now and seeing him with that look on his face as he bent over the hog as he skinned it... it reminded her of a movie she'd watched as a teenager, a scary one. She bit the inside of her cheek, and took another step back. *Why do I feel like I'm interrupting him and that I'm unwelcome?*

A singular force of nature, Elliot hardly fit the traditional mold of a history teacher. His common sense alone, added in with his keen sense of the outdoors, made Ryleigh relax and feel less worried about being stranded. Here, he seemed a natural fit. She was a city mouse, but he was an island mouse.

She trusted Elliot's word that they were safe and that the ship would return soon, and that it was just a matter of time.

TWENTY-NINE
Suffield County Hospital

DETECTIVE CHANDLER walked down the large tiled corridor in the basement of the county hospital, the crepe soles of his topsiders squishing and echoing along the halls. Here, away from the public areas of the hospital, the walls were plain, and some parts still looked like unfinished concrete. He stopped at the door to the morgue. He pulled his coat collar up over his neck.

The Medical Examiner, Tammera, looked up from her glasses as he entered.

Damn it was cold; everything was always absolutely freezing. The first time he'd sat through an autospy, the body had been quite decomposed and he'd been getting sick in his mouth behind his mask, and thinking, "I could never do this job, I'd never be able to deal with the smell." But after a while, he'd stopped noticing it.

As a detective, Chandler was interested in the minutest details about the bodies and what he could discover, but as a person, he was a little embarrassed about the intrusion into the sacred realm of the dead. A morgue wasn't a place he liked to visit, but it was part of the job, so he joked about it. A nervous habit. Jokes kept the mind off other nasty thoughts.

Tammera wore green scrubs, and a clear plastic apron with a large front pocket filled with wads of pink Kleenex. Her black curly hair was covered with a net.

"Chandler, it's great to see you." She walked over and he hugged her.

"Tammy, you're looking well. Either I'm getting older or you are getting younger, but…"

"Quit the bullshit. What brings you here?"

"The cruise ship bodies. All the Americans that died were brought to you."

"I figured they would assign you to the case to investigate it." She walked over to a wall of shiny silver refrigerator drawers, where the bodies were stored before and after they were autopsied.

"Yeah, lucky me, I get all the glamorous accidents. I get to interview all the tan, rich, arrogant passengers for days."

Tammera rolled her eyes and started opening the first compartment after reading the white sticker on the door. She slid out the long tray. The first body was an elderly woman with no signs of trauma to her arms, legs, or torso.

"She was found off the ship?"

"No, in her bed on the ship, the morning after."

"Okay, don't need to see her."

"You said the bodies they brought in from the cruise."

"That I did. I meant the ones found in the water, or on deck, not the ninety-year-old that died peacefully in her sleep from a heart attack."

"She died of cancer."

"Okay, then." He did remember reading that in his files.

"Corpse number two." She slid open another drawer with the petite naked body of a young, freckle-faced, red-head girl. She had large holes in both sides of her swollen, soggy torso, and she was missing her right foot, and four fingers on her right hand; other than that, she looked like she was sleeping.

"Shark attack kill her?" From this vantage point, he couldn't see any other trauma. Such a shame. Someone's cruise had become a horrible nightmare, their always remembering they'd lost a daughter, girlfriend, or sister on the cruise.

"Nope."

"Don't tell me she had cancer, too."

A hint of a smile crossed her face. "No, drowned; there was no evidence whatsoever that her death was due to shark attack. All the other vics' findings indicted postmortem marine animal activity."

"Was she conscious when she hit the water?"

"Yes, signs of water in the lungs. Shark and barracuda bait after she drowned."

"How old was she?"

"Our guess is about seventeen."

"No identification yet?"

"Not this victim. Do you want her on the table?"

"No. Who else you got here?"

Tammera rolled the tray shut, latched the door, and read a few more labels on the next few compartments.

"Two males, both drowned. One sixty-two, the other–"

"–got a girl around thirty-two?"

"No. Why? She still missing?"

"So far, manifest shows she was cleared and left the ship. But I'm not sure. Divers found a pair of shorts with her I.D. in the back pocket. I'm still investigating everyone."

"She just lost the shorts when everything went overboard?"

"You would think. But the shorts ended up on that red-head you just showed me."

"She wasn't wearing them when she came in. She was in a swimsuit." She pulled out a plastic bag from a stack of bins near the coolers. "This was all that was on her." Tammera dumped the contents of the bag onto the table.

He rummaged through the small pile of clothes and a few pieces of jewelry. "Where's the white shorts? They had angel wings or some design on the pockets."

"She didn't have them when she came in."

"Damn. Someone back at the port must have swiped them. That's no way to honor the deceased."

"Chandler, when you've been in this business as long as I have, you wouldn't believe half the stories I could tell you about the ones they bring in here."

"I'm not writing a book. Just investigating the cruise ship accident, and damn, this was supposed to be a simple investigation."

"Mother Nature can be cruel to the human bodies. Do you wanna keep looking at the others?"

"Recovering evidence from the sea can be a bitch. Yep. Let's keep looking. I trust your autopsy reports, but got to verify each and every one."

They spent the next twenty minutes going through the remainder of the cruise ship passengers' bodies. He made notes on his report. Tammera talked the whole time about cruises, vacations, and her German Shepherd, Bear, who was trained to sniff out blood. And how Suffield and Broward County police had borrowed her pup several times. "They said he was better than the academy trained dogs."

"Well, his mom is an M.E. I bet you have lots of samples to train him with."

"Perks of the job."

He was rolling the last corpse into the cooler when Tammera said, "I have one on the table over here. Shark teeth still in his side. Want to help pull them out?" She handed him a pair of silver tongs that looked like large tweezers. She had a grin on her face.

"I'll let you do the honors."

"Thought so." She winked at him.

She talked the whole while she plucked teeth out of the inside flap of the man's midsection. She seemed like the type of mom that could eat a peanut butter sandwich while changing her baby's poopy diaper. She rattled on and on. Her voice shrilled sometimes, then dropped to a whisper among the dead, and then turned shrill again. "Did they find all the bodies?"

"Coast Guard is cruising back and forth where they encountered the waves. There's so many islands and coral reefs in that part of the sea, who knows if they'll find any others?" He examined the large tooth she held in front of him. "Missing four passengers. At least that's all that families and friends and the ship's manifest have confirmed."

For once, she ceased speaking, and her gaze wandered past him, lost in the surrounds of the dead passengers.

THIRTY
Day Seven

ELLIOT STOOD IN the ankle deep water for the second time in thirty minutes, in the small, neat bay, surrounded by rolling hills, mangrove brushes and, of course, palm trees and an unspecified number of birds pecking their way across the beach.

Elliot stared out at the sea. He could never get tired of the majesty of it. It was a textbook day for a deserted island; azure blue painted skies, turquoise seas, sugar crystal beaches, and a surging sea of white capped waves.

Normally, he slept like a rock, but since they'd been stranded, he had slept poorly. Sleep seemed a distant memory, hopefully to return when he got to sleep in a real bed. At least he was used to this life, but not Ryleigh. Poor Ryleigh. How would she have gotten along without him? Considering he was a big part of the reason she was in this mess, he couldn't leave without her knowing how to survive.

The last few days had drifted by, made busy with the many chores that needed to get done. He had patched the holes in the tiki hut, caused by the storm, with new green fronds. He had moved some of the snack bar food and made a covered shelf in the nearby tree that was protected from any wild animals stealing their rations, leaving more room for them to sleep.

He'd set up the fish trap of rocks at the lagoon end of the beach, the boggy area that connected the two islands. So far, he had trapped a few fish that they'd eaten fresh daily. Any smaller ones, he planned to smoke and keep as a reserve.

He had spent many hours making the island more comfortable for Ryleigh. He wanted her to be prepared to survive without him. He smiled when he thought of the two sand dollars she had taped to the portable bathroom doors. Handwritten with a pen from the tiki hut, *men* on one and *Ryleigh* on the other.

"There you are."

He turned around to find Ryleigh wearing an extra-large bright orange souvenir shirt, and he suspected nothing else under it. She had tied a piece of rope around her thinning midsection, using it as a belt. Her hair was tied up high on her head with a piece of strapping from one of the lawn chairs. She looked adorable. Her eyes glimmered green and were thickly lashed in black.

"You look gorgeous, as usual."

"Thank you." Ryleigh swung around, showing off her makeshift dress.

"It's a great day, too. Just look at the blooming greenery up the steep banks."

"Under the circumstances, this is a pretty neat place. There's a sense of tourism in where we are, and yet it's unreal to be here alone. And… Elliot, look!" She pointed toward the horizon.

Elliot saw a helicopter out in the distance. He unconsciously moved closer to the horizon to see it, moving out toward the sea.

"Elliot, the flare guns! What did you do with them?"

Elliot turned and high-kneed it out of the water. Running across the hot sand, he made it to the hut.

Once inside the hut, he immediately put his hand on the flare guns. He grabbed them both, but waited a few seconds before emerging from the hut.

"Elliot, hurry." Ryleigh yelled. "It's turning the other way."

Good, he thought, feeling guilty.

"I've got them. " He came out of the hut and looked toward the horizon. He opened the gun and pretended to be reading the directions on the gun.

"Hurry. Hurry." Ryleigh came running toward him. "Come on. Give it to me."

He pointed it toward the island and shot it off.

They both stared at it, and in the daylight, the orange fumes melted into the yellow sunny skies. The helicopter kept going, away from them.

"Oh no. They're leaving. Come back!" Ryleigh ran into the surf, waving her arms.

Elliot hesitated and, before he knew it, the helicopter was a mere speck on the horizon, but he still shot off the other flare.

He stood there for a moment, looking out across the fathomless bay. "Goodbye," he said at last to the empty horizon.

Ryleigh shook herself and stopped her sweeping arm gestures. She high-kicked and splashed as she made it back to shore.   "You   used   both   flares?"

"I thought…" Elliot didn't finish.

"It's gone," was all she said as she passed Elliot and went toward the hut.

THIRTY-ONE
Dexco Headquarters – Chicago

FOR GREG EDERSOM, it hadn't been a smooth trial. What he'd thought would be an easy litigation process had turned into a major headache. The victims in the class action suit kept coming out of the woodwork.

He heard three fast knocks on the door. "Come in."

"Gregory." A tall, balding man entered his office. Keith Humphrey was the main executive in the pharmaceutical's government department.

"Keith. Have a seat. Do you want a whiskey?"

"No. Thanks. I can't be here long."

"Sure, I understand," Greg said. "What brings you here? You sounded desperate on the phone."

"The documents we thought were hidden seem to have resurfaced. If the prosecutor gets ahold of these, we'll have bigger problems to deal with."

"Which ones?"

"The yearlong clinical trial study."

Dexco's new hit, a diabetes drug that helped with insulin spikes, had been released to the general public last year, after several years in clinical trials.

The data that Dexco had provided to the FDA was based on the first six months during the study, which hadn't shown any deaths. However, the yearlong data had showed the incidents, some resulting in deaths, but these documents had disappeared.

"They're lost, correct?" A worried look crossed Keith's face. Greg saw more lines around his normally smooth, pale skin.

"Yes, the documents are lost, just like the Quality Control Manager that discovered them." Greg looked around the room and then glanced at the door.

"Good, because folks will call that a blatant lie of omission."

"God forbid the press or someone at the FDA got a hold of it."

"We have to keep this under wraps. Only a few people know. We showed our test results, and contrary to what people believed, the FDA doesn't do any testing of drugs that get approved. People don't realize that the FDA has the drug companies pay for and do the studies. The press will have a field day if those deaths can be linked to our new drug. This information can't leak out," Keith said.

"We're probably not the only drug company that submits the good studies that support the release of their drugs."

"But the idea that Dexco withheld critical data, that's a concern." Greg walked over to his large picture window on the 14th floor and looked out.

"But if some of these unsealed documents are found that show this was all part of a carefully calculated plan by Dexco and some of its execs, heads could roll, and stocks plummet," Keith said.

It was true, some of Dexco's medical directors and scientists at the company had expressed feeling uncomfortable with the "data massaging" and "cherry picking" of data, but the powers-that-be had moved full steam ahead with their deceptive marketing releases.

"So we have to make sure that no internal memos make it to the prosecutor's hands." Greg sat behind his desk.

"It won't, right? You said you had taken care of the Quality Manager that found the documents. Ryleigh? Correct?"

"Yes, she's gone for a while during the trial, or maybe forever. She may even be lost at sea or wherever Elliot has put her."

"Lost at sea?" Keith wore a worried look.

"Come on. Keith, relax. We all have an agreement here. Get out of your basement lab once in a while "

The so called powers-that-be had ties to big government and had hired a private investigator, or babysitter, to stay close to one of their own, to make sure she didn't talk. Arrangements had been made over the last year. And just weeks before the trial had started, Ryleigh Lane had left for a long, extended cruise. One that might leave her stranded for the rest of her life.

"Keep me posted on the information they have. I'll check for leaks on this side."

Greg escorted Keith to the door. "You're doing a great job. I hope you're enjoying your new bonus plan."

"Yes, I am."

He closed the door behind him. He wondered if Elliot was enjoying his last date with the cute Quality Control Manager.

THIRTY-TWO
Keg Key

The sun blinked down over the horizon and cast an orange glow across the relatively calm sea. Ryleigh loved the sunsets; she loved just about everything on the island except the part about being stranded... and, well, the food... and the shelter... her clothes and shoes... and many other amenities that she missed, but most of all, she missed her sister and her few friends.

By now, would they be looking for her? She often wondered what was going on back home in Chicago.

For many nights, they fell asleep tightly woven in each other's arms. Ryleigh talked a lot about her family and her last memories of her mom and dad. She had lost details over time, but in her mind she still carried an indelible image of both of them, laughing and loving each other. She remembered constant travel planning, and if they weren't talking about the last trip they had been on, they were talking about the next one they had planned. Such an outlook on traveling must have been useful for operating a travel agency, before Travelocity and Priceline. Ryleigh had finally taken a cruise to some faraway place, something her parents had always encouraged, and with an incredible hunk. She could hear her mom saying, "Way to go, sweetie!"

Now Ryleigh imagined Stuart and May Lane looking down from heaven and whimsically wondering if their oldest twin, by three minutes, had gotten in way over her head. There was no denying the luck of her predicament – a trip to a remote island with an incredible man.

"Aren't you going to finish the calamari?" Elliot picked at a piece of raw tentacle.

Her first bite of raw octopus had tasted pungent and briny. She had resisted a gag.

"I'm used to my sushi with fresh ginger, soy and wasabi. And more time in the refrigerator or spent with the sus chef."

"Aw, understandable. You're not used to the minimal layover between the sea and your mouth? Next time, I will roast it on a stick over the fire. And cut it into thin curls."

"I look forward to that," she yawned. "I'm exhausted."

They had just finished dinner and Ryleigh wanted to go to bed early, after the sunset. They often played Gin Rummy at night with the deck of cards Elliot had found in the backpack. She had never played before, but he'd taught her. She still hadn't won a game.

"Elliot, do you have friends that would be looking for you? Besides work?" She knew he was off school for the summer, and he didn't need to report to anyone. He'd told her before that he often went sailing or on excursions all summer, so no one would be looking for him.

"No, I told you, I go away most summers, so I doubt that anyone is worried about me."

"Not a close friend?"

He shook his head.

"None?" she asked. She wanted to think he had a close buddy at home worried about him. That would be a fine character reference.

"I really don't have time for close friends. I have my work acquaintances, but they're not really close. We go out and blow off steam after work, but that's it."

"No one who'll worry you were lost at sea?"

"No; maybe when school starts in September."

Her eyes drifted shut. "Oh."

"Did you like dinner? You barely touched it." Elliot asked, changing the subject. In addition to the octopus, he had placed three finger-size strips of grilled fish on her plate, and breadfruit, and she had only eaten one piece of fish.

The wind picked up, swirling the hot, humid air along the beach, and the coconut trees over the lawn chairs creaked nosily. A night bird made a raucous noise, startling her. She craned her neck forward and peered into the dark woods; it went silent. She turned back to Elliot. "I'm not hungry tonight."

"Ryleigh, you need to eat. To keep up your strength. I can hunt another hog tomorrow. You loved the meat."

She had enjoyed the many meals they'd gotten from the hog, before it went rancid. Without refrigeration, they never ate the same animal, bird or fish or otherwise, for more than a day or two. "I'm just tired. That's all. I think I'll retire to the hut."

"Okay. I'll join you a little later."

Ryleigh stood up and leaned over to kiss Elliot, but he wore a worried look.

"Let me check it out before you do," he said with a chilling finality, as if there could be rats, snakes, and bugs sleeping in their straw bed.

He jumped up and strode to the hut. Oh, how she loved her Hunk-a-berry guy. He was her protector, her lover, her best friend, her chef, her hunter... her everything.

"All clear," Elliot said when he returned. In the moonlight and the faint glow of the fire pit, Elliot looked delicious even in his signature island garb; camouflage shorts held up by a rope belt, tan body, and aqua eyes set against his chiseled face. The island food and daily chores had worn well on him. They suited Elliot, and he looked comfortable in their new life.

She reached for his hand, and she pulled him toward the hut. "Join me?"

117

"I'll join you in a little while."

She was disappointed, and when she glanced her questioning eyes to Elliot, he didn't even look her way, all his attention on the darken horizon instead.

She sighed and straightened, "Then I'll see you in a few." She felt the small calluses that had formed on his palm beneath his fingers. All the hard work he had done to make their stranded life on a deserted island more palatable.

When he turned toward her, there was a pained look in his eyes, one that sent sadness rippling through her. He nodded and let go of her hand.

As she lay in their makeshift bed, Ryleigh could hear waves outside the hut, breaking on the sand, which until weeks ago had been a completely foreign sound. Now she'd grown so accustomed to the sounds that she wondered if she'd ever fall asleep without them. She felt a little sick and wondered if it was time for her period.

Ryleigh had horrible menstruating periods that left her cramping in the hut for hours. So far, that had only happened once since they'd come to the island. Her period was almost nothing at all, but its scantiness was completely regular each month.

Her period had ended on the first day of the cruise. And she and Elliot now had unprotected sex several times a day and night. She made love with him more than she had anyone else in her life.

But when she'd been born, she had had some hormonal issues, and she'd once been told she would need state-of-the-art assistance to ever get pregnant. Even if the test tube baby were to work, genetically and physically, she would be at high risk. She knew she couldn't get pregnant. She had discussed it with

Elliot early in their courting days, and he hadn't seemed too worried. *Not a fatherly type?*

Ryleigh, not as tired as she'd thought, tossed and turned and fell in and out of sleep. She turned over, suddenly awakening in excruciating pain and, with the light from the flashlight, she discovered she had a strange mark on her left wrist. The spot on her arm reddened and swelled up before her eyes.

"Elliot, help me!" She yelled as she lay on her back, staring at the thatched roof forming a cold, bleak shelter over her head, and she felt what could only be snake venom beginning to take effect. Gradually, what felt like a hand squeezed her lungs, forcing her to breathe in shallow gasps. Would this sensation spread to her heart? She felt her chest constricting. Would she become paralyzed?

She drifted. "Elliot..." Everything clouded over.

Ryleigh, you'll be fine... I have experience... lay still...

There was only pain. Her arm stung. Her tongue was swollen in her throat, dry and sour. Her head was throbbing, her body bathed in sweat.

Ryleigh found herself on a flowered mountainside. The sun was burning proud and the wind was idle. The first thing that Ryleigh recognized was the ugly tiki hut, torn and battered. Before she could orient herself on the mountain, she heard a woman's cry, and the sucking sound of hundreds of leaches. Her heartbeat quickened, as she raced to the hut and entered, and saw Elliot bent over a beautiful, naked tanned woman, his mouth sucking her wrist. And blood everywhere.

There was something familiar about the woman. It took several seconds for her to grasp that the woman lying in Elliot's grip was in fact herself, Ryleigh.

Through the fog, she heard Elliot.

"Ry, you're going to be okay. I'm taking care of the poison."

Then the sucking leaches sound, and the blood, her blood, everywhere. She spiraled down the tunnel again and his voice was soothing. His hands comforting her. Wet rags on her forehead.

Oh Elliot, my Hunk-le-berry Finn, is now Dr. Hunkaberry.

"Ryleigh, you're doing great. Hang in there, babe. Please." Ryleigh heard his garbled voice.

She opened her eyes. "I have to pee."

"Baby, how are you? And don't get up just yet." Elliot's voice was choked and he looked relieved.

"I seriously have to go the bathroom; my head is sore like a hellava hangover and my arm feels like I pitched a no-hitter for the Cubs." He kissed her forehead and she responded by trying to lift her left arm to run her hand through his hair.

"Ow."

"Slowly. Watch the arm."

Ryleigh leaned forward and arched her back, and then scooted forward.

"That's my girl. Sit up, careful." He helped her to sit up and lean against the hut wall.

"What happened?" Her throat felt dry and her voice sounded raspy. There were t-shirts with blood stains everywhere, and her left wrist was wrapped in a white piece of cloth and tied with a piece of rope.

"Darling, you were bitten by a snake. And you passed out."

She saw the light streaming through the hut, and Elliot's hair disheveled. "You stayed up all night with me?"

"Yes, of course, both nights."

"What? How long was I asleep?"

"A few days. Here, drink a sip of water." He picked up a plastic bottle, with some of the remaining fresh bottled water, and placed it to her trembling lips.

Days? Her Dr. Hunkleberry had nursed her for days? Her eyes warm with tears, a lump filled her throat.

He sighed and tucked her loose wild hair behind her ear.

"Oh no, was it poisonous?"

"To your body, yes. Snake venom effects people different ways. Like bee stings. But you're better, that's all that matters."

"Let me see it." She removed the blood-stained t-shirt from her arm and there were two small holes by her left wrist. "Looks like I tried to commit suicide."

"Those are the fang marks…" he said it painfully.

"Did you suck the venom? I had dreams about leaches."

"No, sucking is folklore. Or at least, if I don't want the toxin in my blood stream, sucking the venom is not too smart."

"Really? I would have thought that's what you're supposed to do, but that probably is the Red Cross advice for snake-bitten hikers at the turn of the century."

"Especially if there's not a hospital in sight, or antivenin." She couldn't believe there had been a snake in the hut, since Elliot had checked it. "Did you see it?"

"No, it must have crawled in and out before I got to you." He pointed at a few of the bloody shirts. It's better to let the wound naturally bleed out, and unfortunately, the strike hit your vein, causing spurting blood.

"I'm never going to feel safe again on this island of snakes. I'm a city dweller and I used to worry about being mugged on Michigan Avenue or the El, and I have three deadbolts on my townhouse door, but here, I have new worries." Tears slid down her face and she buried her head into Elliot's chest.

"You're safe now. You're going to be alright," he murmured into her hair, his voice hoarse. "Don't cry, Ryleigh."

She smoothed her fingers over his stubble. They looked to be two of the same, dirty and upheaved. Smelly.

"We stink," she laughed. "And I must look like a train wreck."

"Let me help you stand. Let's go take a salt water shower. Then we can gorge on mangoes."

And for the moment, she thought that was the most logical thing to do, in their absurd situation called life.

THIRTY-THREE
Day Twenty-One

A SMALL WAVE building ten feet away crashed down on them, knocking them to their knees and leaving them drenched.

Ryleigh worked her way back to her feet, "Okay. Enough." She was playful, winded, but felt more relaxed than she had in the last few weeks. "Enough."

Elliot came at her again. Putting her on her back, holding her there, until the wave came.

"No more, Elliot, stop it," she said, choking up water as she dog-paddled, trying to catch her breath until her knees scraped the shore. They worked hard on the island, they played hard, and as always, the sex was great. Even though they'd been thrown into their life together, they still found excitement and mystery and hunger between them, always fueling their passion for each other.

Elliot was on his feet, and he grabbed her, careful not to touch her left wrist where the mark was red, but fading, and for a moment, she thought he was going to knock her into the wave again, but suddenly the waves and the water, the silly game they were playing – all of it was forgotten.

"Look!" Ryleigh took a few large steps, parallel to the surf, not noticing the salty spray in her face. She pointed at the horizon.

Elliot stopped splashing. "Ryleigh, I swear you're a poor loser..." He stopped, turned around, and peered toward the horizon.

"What's that?" Elliot hurried his steps out to the sea. He squinted in the same direction as Ryleigh.

"No..." Elliot slowed his steps. "The flags, "he hesitated, "that isn't good. Pirates?"

"It's a rescue boat!" She had never given up hope that a rescue boat would still come, but when the days had turned to weeks, and the weeks now almost a month, she'd wondered if they really were lost from society. "Elliot, even if it's not our rescue boat, it's a way off this island."

Together, they raced to shore, while their jaw-dropped glances kept going back to the boat. Ryleigh grabbed her swimsuit bottoms and slipped them on. *Why does Elliot look nervous?* The silhouette of the ship was ominous, warlike. And suddenly she felt like they had been caught in a sea battle without any weapons or any form of protection.

"You're right, we shouldn't panic, but still be concerned."

"Panic?"

"Ryleigh, those flags are hard to see; I'll get the binoculars."

Excitement and fear choked out every wonderful thing Ryleigh had been feeling moments earlier. She shaded her eyes, watching the large ship. She squinted at Elliot, "You're serious?"

He grabbed her arm and pulled her. "Come on."

The ship had turned toward the island and was closing in.

"Let's get to the hut so I can grab the binoculars."

Weeks earlier, they had never left their excursion beach without the binoculars, knife, and flare gun. Now they were steps away from the hut and they needed to see what was out there.

Pulling her along, Elliot began jogging through the hot, thick sand, and somehow she matched his pace.

"Hurry."

Her heart pounded, she was so excited to see a ship, or was it nervousness over who was on the ship?

"Ryleigh, we have no need to be scared." Elliot was yelling back at her.

"Another ship!"

Nearly an hour had passed and the two ships had stayed on the horizon, and now as the sun dipped into the ocean, the flowing tide swept through the narrow space between the pier pilings in little waves of seething foam, and Ryleigh, with one long look at the ships through the binoculars, sighed, "Damn it, do I have to stay hidden?"

Elliot was pacing the sand-beaten path behind the hut, out of sight of the ships, talking to himself. He looked over at her, "You realize they could be our saviors or our executioners?"

"If they're pirates, will they capture us, rob us, eat us…?"

Elliot stared at her. "They may rob and rape, but pirates aren't cannibals."

"That's comforting."

"Just stay close. I'll watch the horizon for now. This could be the greatest moment for us since three weeks ago – our way off the island may be waiting out there."

"I wish we had the flare gun," she said reluctantly, without trying to point blame. The flare gun episode was still a sore spot in their minds.

Elliot gave her a look with flaring nostrils. Like he had that night. His face turned red even in the glow of the setting sun, and he looked cross. So here they were once again, her looking frightened and upset, and him just pissed off. The air between them was charged, as they both had something weighing on their minds and neither could push past the awkwardness. His stern features chiseled his face, indicating he was troubled.

"Elliot, I didn't mean to bring it up."

"But you're right. I fucked up. I said it that night, I wasted our flares."

"We wouldn't need them anyway, not now. Not until we're sure if these boats are friendly or not. I agree with you, they don't look like tourists," she said as she walked the sandy path with him, a new thought forming within her. *Did he intentionally use the flares?* He's a smart guy and he knew they were necessary to have.

She looked over at Elliot. The thought of him lying or deceiving her left her hurting. Somehow, even now, the thought of his intentions seemed wrong; why? Her practical side couldn't fathom it, but like the air they breathed, it just was. *What else is he hiding?*

Well, she hadn't been so honest herself. He had to have questions about her, too, and she had a feeling she couldn't answer them honestly. Not yet.

THIRTY-FOUR

A COOL WIND whipped through the sands near the hut, waking him. The gust of sand felt coarse as it brushed across his flesh. He rubbed the few grains out of his long chin stubble. He hadn't shaved his facial stubble in a week, as he wanted to preserve the few blue plastic razors in the hut's toiletries for Ryleigh. She seemed more self-conscious about her hairy arm pits and legs. Besides, his scattering of facial hair was a golden mask that spread across his cheeks and chin, creeping down his tan neck. If he let it grow out, he wondered if it could cover so much of his face that only his nose and blue eyes would be visible, and when he devoured raw fish, his beard would be tangled and grimy with fish guts.

Would his beard mold, like a dirty kitchen sponge? He cupped his chin in his hand, and kicked the sand into the small fire in front of him, putting it out immediately.

The sandy binoculars perched on his eyes reminded him of another day and time. A time when he'd had no one. Now he had Ryleigh. He trusted Ryleigh, didn't he?

You didn't last long in his profession if you didn't trust anyone. If you're too busy looking over your shoulder, you can't see far enough in front of you to see what's coming at you.

He had Ryleigh now to protect.

The smoke from the squelched fire filled his nose and he resisted sneezing, afraid to wake Ryleigh, who was sleeping peacefully in the hammock slung beneath the leafy mango trees.

On some level, he knew his world was hopelessly out of sync, as if he'd been caught between two dimensions and he was unable to live completely yet in either one. Logically, he was sure there had to be a way back to his life – he could escape. Or had he?

If only there was more he could do.

As if she heard his thoughts, his gaze caught Ryleigh tumbling out of the hammock and wandering to him.

"Hey, babe, sorry I fell asleep. Any signs of the ships moving?"

"They're a little closer to the islands and they're not firing machine guns or cannons at us, so that's good."

"Should we signal them then? And see if they can take us out of here?"

"Ry, I'm not sure if they're friendly."

"It's not like we have a bunch of boats and helicopters to choose from."

"You got a point there. They're not exactly lining up and knocking themselves out to find us, are they now?"

"Right? You know I'd give my left kidney for a real shower and a spa."

"That's all?" He pulled her close.

"Well, that and maybe a gallon of Rocky Road ice cream."

"Come on, how bad can it be here?"

"We're stranded on a remote island with no running water, no electricity, no real food, and plenty of bugs and snakes... it can be better!"

She leaned into him and opened her mouth on top of his, and he closed his eyes and darted his tongue into her mouth, feeling her hands wrap around his.

Ryleigh lured the binoculars out of his hands.

"Hmm, if you wanted the binoculars, you could have just asked," he whispered in her hair.

"But this is much more fun." Her grin melted his heart every time.

"Indeed." He kissed her again.

Ryleigh brushed the sand off the lens, and squinted as she brought the black plastic lens to her eyes.

Elliot followed her direction. The ocean was dark midnight blue, large white caps topping the waves, a black silhouette of the ships floating on the horizon – it all looked like it had been photographed for a pirate movie trailer.

"Do you see them?"

"Yes. What should we do? A fire?"

"I've been thinking a lot about it. And after reading about drug kingpins, I don't think it's a wise idea to just attract them, do you?" Elliot hoped she'd see the danger in it, before making a judgment. Some of her hasty food decisions almost left her with a bad stomachache. Her lapse of good judgments clouded decisions here in isolation, alone, removed from a life she knew in Chicago, and he'd worried it would drive them both nuts.

"There's got to be something we can do besides just wait."

"If they were closer, I could see all the flags. My concern is that to operate a ship on these seas with fewer regulations or controls can lead to piracy."

"Really?"

"At sea, the laws are set forth by the maritime laws of the nearest country. So, for example, a U.S. ship near the Bahamas follows the Bahamian law."

"Either way, laws or maritime laws, it's just the humane thing to do, to save stranded souls."

"True, you would think, but regardless of humanity or legal recourse, or what's ethical or not, if we're dealing with modern-day pirates, we could be screwed."

"I just don't understand how you know so much. First a Russian plane, and now ships. How does a guy with a PhD in sociology with a focus on–"

Elliot finished her sentence, "–focus on nonviolent alternatives to war."

"Whatever. Sweetheart, you just perplex me sometimes, a know-it-all."

Elliot frowned.

She continued, "but in a good way."

"I told you I knew about the Russian plane because of a cruise I took on the Mikhail Lermontar, from a U.S. port." He hated lying again to her. It was complicated, and to keep her curiosity at bay, he had to throw tidbits to her. Ryleigh was smart and beautiful, and with each day they spent alone on the island, he gained a deeper understanding of her, and her well-concealed inner side, as well.

"But you said the only security out at sea were the ship's security officers. Can't we at least try to signal them?"

"I remember reading, before the cruise, that this area is famous for pirate-infested waters, and they terrorize the small crafts on the seas."

"Just our fucking luck! We see not one, but two ships, signaling-distance away, and we can't even call them, because we're concerned that instead of saving us, they'll rape and murder us."

He gathered her in his arms and smoothed her fly-away strands of hair off her face. "My sweet sea gypsy, I don't want to risk you, us, this–"He swung his free arm around, pointing at the island. "Why ruin our quiet refuge just yet?"

It was getting hotter and the sun was hidden behind a dark bank of clouds. He wondered how long they could hide at night without lighting the fire.

She flinched and her dark eyes widened.

Now what?

"Elliot, turn around, they're moving this way!"

130

THIRTY-FIVE

THE TWO SHIPS moved easily across the bay side of Keg Key, and as they approached, Elliot grabbed the duffle bag and a knapsack. The bag's insides were moving.

"Elliot, what the hell is in that bag?"

"I've been hunting a few hungry critters for a time like this," he said as he grabbed the rope holding the bag closed and proceeded to cut it open. "Grab that smaller bag."

They were near the hut, Ryleigh thought. *Have the bags been behind the hut all this time?* She couldn't keep her eyes off the bag Elliot held.

"What kind of critters?" She glared at him stonily.

"We don't have much time. Open your bag and dump the contents around the hut floor.

Ryleigh opened the smaller bag, peered inside, and screamed. "Elliot, where did you get all these bugs and dead mice?"

"They're dead? Damn. Come on, Ryleigh, we don't have all day."

She slowly dumped the contents out.

"Hurry, they're almost to shore." Elliot grabbed the smaller bag out of her hands, placing the larger one filled with God-knew-what on the ground, and poured out the contents.

Beetles, worms, roaches, and a few staggering live mice scattered around the floor of the hut and spilled out to the pier.

Ryleigh put her hand to her mouth, taking three small steps backwards. Her eyes were wide. What was Elliot thinking? What did these bugs have to do with their hut and the boats heading their way? But before she had the courage to speak, Elliot burst out orders.

"Get back. Don't go the beach route to the lagoon trail. Go this way, behind the hut." He pointed toward a path less traveled by both of them.

Elliot slowly opened the other bag. "Keep back: these mothers will be angry, hungry, and moving."

He didn't have to ask Ryleigh twice when he dumped a bag of snakes onto the floorboard. He held a few wiggling creatures in the bag back and dumped them near the entrance to the hut.

"Mother F'ing God." Ryleigh ran to the trail Elliot had told her to go toward. She looked around her feet and stomped up and down. She felt like bugs and snakes were crawling up her legs.

Within seconds, Elliot joined her.

"Why are we running? We need to stay and get rescued. This doesn't feel like the best plan."

"I recognize the boat and symbols. Not good." He stopped and looked into her eyes, "Trust me?"

She wanted to. She broke out in a sweat. Not being in control of a situation was always one of her biggest fears, and since getting stranded on the island, she'd felt she had no control. Elliot had controlled everything. Where they slept. What they ate. How they signaled for help. Everything. And with that control, she gave a level of trust. Had he steered her wrong yet?

When she didn't respond, he grabbed her hand and pulled her into the mangrove brush. He had the backpack strapped around his bare back. "Follow me. We have to hide. Do exactly as I do. Each step you take, follow me in my footprints, mimic me."

"Okay." She was short of breath and her legs were wobbly, but she followed Elliot closely, mirroring every movement, still feeling uneasy about hiding. Why was this the best option?

They walked for five minutes. They weren't very far into the forest because they moved with purpose. Each step careful not to break a branch or leave a print. Around them, the island jungle was full of insects rubbing their wings and singing.

"Here, get down on all fours." Elliot pointed toward the matted grassy path.

"Where are we?"

"Trust me."

That was the second time he'd asked. Or was that a command and not a question? That was a valid question; did she trust him? She got down on all fours.

Elliot knelt down alongside her and moved a few palm fronds and hollow trunks. To the normal eye, all she saw was rocks and a wall of trees pushed up to the side of a berm.

Slowly, as Elliot moved the shrubbery, a tiny opening about the size of a manhole cover appeared. "Oh geez. Are we going in there?"

"Yes. Get on your belly and slither in."

She hesitated and, with every ounce of courage she had left in her, she fell to a planking position and pulled her body forward. "How do you know what's in there? Are you coming, too?"

"It's a cave; I discovered it recently. When you get inside, you can sit up. Stay to the left wall, right inside the door. I'll cover the door with brush back behind you. I'm going to go back and see if they're friendly or not."

Ryleigh bent over and gripped Elliot's hand. "I want to stay with you. Is this all necessary? Can't we just watch and see who comes to the camp? Maybe they'll rescue us and–"

Gunshots blasted in the distance, coming from the camp.

"Get in. Now!"

"But who are they shooting–?"

"–the snakes. They're in our hut."

"No. I'm coming with you." She couldn't stand the thought of hiding in a cave, not knowing what was happening. She'd rather be in danger than left alone in a small cave, waiting anxiously to know what had happened.

Elliot grabbed her shoulders and stared firmly in her eyes. "You have to wait here. We only have one knife, and I can't fight off the bad guys if I'm trying to defend you, as well. Now get in the cave before I drag you in there."

Ryleigh slithered forward, groping the sandy floor of the small cave opening. The further she went in, the darker and cooler it got. Finally, she was able to sit up. Goosebumps covered every inch of her body and the tiny hairs on her skin were standing straight up.

She dared not feel around because of the possibility that she shared the cave with rats, bats, or worst of all, snakes. She saw Elliot covering the cave opening and the last bit of sunlight diminished to a few slivers of pearly rays sneaking through the fanned leaves of the palm throngs.

"I'll be back in thirty minutes; if I'm not back by then, wait thirty more and then come looking for me. Got it?"

"Really? An hour in here? Come back with good news. I'm ready for a soft bed soon. Be careful, sweetheart."

He didn't say anything else. His shadow moved away from the opening and she sat in the dark, silent cave. She pulled her knees to her chest and wrapped her arms around them. Rocking back and forth. Staring into the dark, trying to make out any movements. The evening was hot, the cave air moist and heavy with the scent of dozens of shelter-seeking varmints.

How would she know when an hour had gone by? She started counting to herself. *One Mississippi. Two Mississippi. Three Mississippi.*

THIRTY-SIX

ELLIOT SHIMMIED UP the breadfruit tree, careful not to shake one branch, not even one leaf.

He found the board he had carefully nailed in place for the lookout. He positioned his back against the widest part of the trunk of the tree and balanced his feet on the board.

With a smooth transition, he swung the binoculars hanging off his backpack to the front and pulled them into place. As planned, he had a clear view to the camp and the open sea beyond their beach.

One ship was leaving, and he could see the shadow of it on the horizon. That might be good. If they were friendly, negotiating with one captain would be easier for him.

"One on deck, two on ground, three in water," he said softly out loud. He counted ten men total. Make that eleven. One man lay in the sand outside the hut door. He pressed his black bandana to his calf.

Through the binoculars, he could read the lips of the man laying closest to him on the ground.

"Cap, was it poisonous? Will I die?"

The man he talked to had his arms full of bagged chips and some toiletries from the hut. Elliot couldn't see his face when he responded.

But he read snake-bitten-man's lips as he replied. *"It's killing me. The pain is fucking terrible. I told you assholes this is Culebra Island, Snake Island. Ten snakes for every foot of island. Big boas drop out of the trees and strangle men and eat them whole. Help me to the ship. Let's get the hell out of here."*

The Captain dropped his supplies and pulled out a gun.

Elliot didn't have to read the wounded man's lips; he could tell he was pleading for his life.

The first shot he took, he fired at the man's wounded calf. Several other men checking out the beach heard the shot and came running toward the hut. The second shot was at snake-bitten man's chest. A large red stain formed on his white t-shirt.

Elliot couldn't read any of the others' lips, but they were all shouting, and a shuffle broke out between two of the men. One of them was holding off the other, from the apparent captain.

Just as Elliot had suspected, modern day pirates. They didn't come equipped with swords or wear eye patches: they drove fast boats and used guns. They weren't too smart and usually robbed vacationers and murdered everyone on the yachts, or in some cases they kidnapped the rich ones for ransom.

He waited for the rest of the crew to grab their dead traveling companion. He figured they would toss him over to the sharks, once they got out to the open sea.

As quickly as they had landed on the island, they swiftly took off. Many of them had been afraid to go in the hut to gather even the smallest of supplies, and had left empty-handed.

The men waded back to their dingy and pointed toward the ship. They left their comrade lying in the sand near the hut. One man remained to clean up the mess.

The men in the dingy scanned the island. Elliot ducked down low in the tree. After a few minutes, he sat up and peered through the binoculars. There was a huge, dark man posted on the bow, scanning the island. Elliot remained still. The white sand was turning red around the body lying near the hut.

One single man stood on the beach, looking out into the brush. He yelled back to the dingy boat, "Come back for me in five minutes; I gotta take a leak."

That was Elliot's sign. He jumped out of the tree and made his way toward the tiki hut.

He knew it had been over thirty minutes and he hoped Ryleigh stayed put while he rushed back to the camp and negotiated with the sole man on the beach. He didn't want her to see what would transpire between them.

THIRTY-SEVEN

RYLEIGH'S HEART POUNDED. She stopped counting after a few minutes. She felt around the cave and, after her eyes adjusted, she saw shadows of ferns or roots hanging from the shallow ceiling. The cave couldn't be more than four feet tall.

She had no idea how deep it went.

"Elliot, hurry back," she said to the empty cave and didn't hear an echo – probably not that deep.

Ryleigh heard several gunshots. She prayed they were killing more snakes. She prayed Elliot was safe. Ryleigh's imagination grappled with the surrounding sounds of the cave, the island, and the pirates invading their camp. She was a city person and had always been a city person. She had never even spent a week in a tent. Now she lived on a beach without plumbing and was hiding in a shallow cave. She was aware of every breath she took, cognizant of the heat.

How long had she been waiting? When was the last time she'd heard the gunshots?

"Damn him for leaving me behind. Elliot Finn can be overbearing, bossy, unrelenting sometimes."

She sat with her senses alert, her mind running, wildly active. How long had he been gone? He'd said he'd return in an hour, but she didn't plan to give him that much time. Thirty minutes, tops. But what if he lay dying somewhere and she could help him? Should she go now? Screw waiting for him.

She sat for a few more minutes, justifying her early exit from the cave, and then she saw the ferns move. With her elbows pressed to her sides, she made her body as small as possible, blinking rapidly as she tried to see who was at the opening. She held her breath.

"It's all right," Elliot said as he stood outside the cave entrance. "They're gone."

Ryleigh exhaled. "Were they bad guys? Were they shooting snakes? I heard two shots."

"No, they killed one of their own."

"Really? Geez. You saw it?"

"Yes." He grabbed her clammy hands and tugged her out and to her feet.

When she could stand on her own, she jumped into Elliot's embrace. "Oh, Elliot, I thought, you were shot." She collapsed in his arms and they clung together without speaking.

Tears slid down her cheeks. "So they're gone? All of them?" A dose of fear mixed with adrenaline quickly cleared her body.

"Yes, they're gone."

"What took you so long?" She felt the first twinges of total loss without him. How could she have ever managed without this man?

"I had a mess to clean up at the camp."

"I would have helped."

"No, this wasn't ladies' work."

She stopped walking and let go of his hand. "Elliot, I'm a lot stronger than you make me out to be."

"I'm sorry; I didn't mean to insult you, but they left something behind that I needed to bury."

"You're right. I couldn't handle that. Thank you." She shivered in the sunshine. "What were they here for? Did you hear or see them? Could we have stolen their boat?"

"Ryleigh, they're killers. I'm not too sure of why they were here." He kicked at the sand trail as he looked at his feet. "They ransacked the hut and left."

"That's why you released those snakes?"

"Yes, madam."

"Hunk-a-berry Finn, you are full of surprises."

"Elliot Finn to you, miss."

"Well, Elliott Hunk Finn, there's no one around to rob or ransack, so it surprises me they even stopped here, so I thought maybe they came to see what the cruise ship left."

"No, that wouldn't be worth the costs of gas."

"That's reassuring."

"Sorry, but we're so remote, no one will plan to come here, unless there's something more."

"Like what? A treasure?"

He raised his eyebrows and his forehead wrinkled. They had made it back to the clearing toward the camp. The sun was beginning its ascent, the rays reflecting off the empty horizon. Clearly, no more boats.

She didn't give the topic a rest. "That's so unreal. You really don't believe in that hidden treasure stuff?"

"I don't. But many do. There have always been theories about treasures in these areas. The same mystery has surrounded the islands for centuries."

It seemed a bitter irony to Ryleigh that if they found something of value, like treasure, she would gladly give it up to be back home safely.

THIRTY-EIGHT

THE MONTH CAME to an end, and still no signs of rescue. Ryleigh kicked up sand as she tromped along the shore, like she did with the snow on the grass in Chicago. She was falling in deep for Elliot, but hated what life with him had become, and cursed herself for thinking that everything was his fault.

For once, in many days and nights, Ryleigh actually looked forward to this day of the week. Lately, the days for Ryleigh and Elliot were starting to become routine. Set chores each day. Desalinate the water. Huckleberry Elliot had thought of that. Some contraption of plastic rafts and containers catching the water as it evaporated. Rain water was plentiful on the island, as well. Their chores kept them busy for the most part. Catch fish or shell fish. Keep the fire lit. Explore the island. Gather fruits. Mend the hut. Check the bird traps.

It wasn't the way Ryleigh would have chosen to spend their days on a beautiful, tropical island, but it kept them busy. Gone were the days of fighting rush hour traffic, running errands on her lunch breaks, all day meetings and constant appointments. She discovered she'd become accustomed to the solitude and isolation of the life they now led. She was at odds with the Chicago life she'd once left behind, and if they were rescued and their stranded adventure was over, Ryleigh doubted she'd ever go back to her old lifestyle in Chicago.

Besides their daily chores, their time here had also been filled with fun, and growing admiration and trust for each other. Ryleigh was continually amazed at Elliot's ingenuity and adaptability, at his dogged courage and his forever encouraging spirit. Sometimes it was a chore just for her to get out of the hammock.

"There you are." She walked up behind him.

141

"Hey there. Are you excited for our fishing trip tonight?" He was piling additional rocks along the Y that he had built at the end of the beach where fish would get trapped. The primitive, but ingenious funnel-shaped lure sucked water in where fish of all sizes would go to feed, and then have difficulty escaping.

It had been a constant source of fresh fish.

Huckleberry Elliot, or *Castaway* Tom Hanks, as she sometimes called him, had snares and traps set up all over the small part of the island.

Most of the time he was naked, except for a belt that held his knife sheath and a small canvas cloth. Today, he wore the long pair of camouflage shorts he'd found in the backpack behind the hut. They were too small around the waist, so he left them unbuttoned and used rope as a belt to keep them from falling completely off. Elliot's island uniform, which she'd once thought sexy, was now beginning to look frayed and worn, even though they both washed what little clothes they had with the dish soap the chefs had left in the hut. She even washed her hair with a few drops of commercial-grade dish soap.

"I'm as excited as a kid on Christmas morning."

"I love that. We can leave for the other end after we eat. Make sure to cover up with bug spray."

Ryleigh had been careful and not too generous with the toiletries left in the hut. They had begun to ration everything after the first week of being stranded. The pirates' pillaging had left them with even less inventory, making their reserve smaller.

"What should we do before dinner? I'm so excited for a lobster dinner that I need something to keep me preoccupied."

"I could make a raft, like that Tom character."

"Tom Sawyer, in *Huckleberry Finn*?" Ryleigh watched him walk over to the line of palm trees where the smooth beach ended abruptly and the woods began.

The thought of Elliot making a raft made her smile, and for a moment reflect on the ambience of the place they were stuck at. It was exotic and full of charm, redolent of island life, and very far removed from all that characterized back home.

She watched Elliott gather up long palm branches. Oddly enough, he could hardly have been more out of place; yet, he didn't look it at all. She admired him.

She reflected on home. Her life uneventful, except for the secrets. The drug company lies. The terrible things that might happen if... if she didn't help. She thought about the small yellow wood-framed house on Central Street. Her lonely and unromantic home on Central. She had grown up and lived there for sixteen years until she'd left for college.

"Come on, Ryleigh." Elliot yelled, waving a palm branch gathered from the forest floor.

Why not? One of the great features of the island, it had infused its own strong individuality into them, and absorbing new ideas of survival that had taken firm hold of her mind had given her such a consciousness of the divine presence.

"I think you meant Tom Hanks, in *Castaway*, not Tom Sawyer." She joined him at the edge of the woods.

"Yep. That one. The one that survived the cargo plane crash?" He didn't look up as he picked up another palm branch.

"Fed ex."

He stopped and tilted his head as he looked her way.

There I go again, always correcting him on trivial matters.

As if he read her thoughts, he said, "Yay, yay, Fed Ex. You are the movie buff."

"He did make a cool raft from the airplane wing. It took him a long time to figure it all out. We'll be rescued before then."

The armful of palm branches fell softly to the sand as he released them. "And we don't have a metal wing as the base."

Ryleigh dropped the one measly palm branch on his pile and wrapped her arms around his upper chest. "We'll figure something out. Forget the raft for now; let's go play in the hut."

THIRTY-NINE

THEY MADE the two hour hike to the outer side of Keg Key where they could see Snake Island, Bird Island, and a few smaller sandbars. Since being left behind on Keg Key, they hadn't returned to a sandbar, of which there were plenty. They had made-up names for all the islands and sandbars that surrounded them.

"Is the moon right tonight, Hunk-a-berry?" She squeezed his hand. A board bank of rolling clouds allowed only brief glimpses of the rising moon.

"So I'm a hunk, tonight?"

"Every day and night."

"Tonight, we have absolutely perfect conditions. Third quarter of a moon. Tide receded, less water around the reefs."

"I wish we had two underwater flashlights." It had been a sore spot for Ryleigh that Elliot had taken control of the items left behind in the hut. He controlled the flashlight, the snorkels, the inner tube, the fins, the knife.... Not that she didn't trust him; she just wished she had more control. But he was always right. His familiarity with nature and hunting and survival was uncanny. Hers, awkward. He was inventive and ingenious. She was inept when it came to all things outdoors.

"Here we are." Elliot stopped at the entrance of the shore closest to the coral reef.

The island served up plenty of adventure and sweet solitude. Her heart soared. She was excited to catch and eat lobster, but the vulnerability of being under the sea at night, hunting and dislodging the spiny crustaceans, created a stampede of panic. Which, up until twenty-nine days ago, was not an emotion she had felt before in her otherwise calm world; being afraid of sea creatures seemed less threatening than the pharmaceutical thugs always watching and keeping her townhouse under surveillance.

Her fear of her predicament back home the last few weeks had dissipated somewhat, and given way to anger.

Within fifteen minutes, they descended into the deep water, looking for lobsters while the last of the sun set on the horizon. The water was naked, clear, and black. The ocean floor looked like a barrel of tar. Ryleigh blinked her eyes, wondering what else lingered in the treacherous night waters. They were swimming into a perpetual night.

Probing the chilly depths like Jacques Cousteau, the two swam deeper into the darkening sea. Their lungs allowed them forty-five seconds of wonderment before they had to surface to let their snorkels clear. They felt at home in the water, not realizing that trouble could be waiting for them at every turn. Trouble wasn't as much of a concern in their lives now. Having had to battle pirates, drug lords, snakes, sharp coral, elements – at every turn – life on the island could encompass trouble.

Eerie shadows in the wilderness of the sea, and a spherical shape moved slowly toward the surface. As it slithered closer to the surface, the ghostly glimmer of the late day outlined its shape.

Half-hidden in the dark waters, scanning the scene, the predator moved into their vision. Slowly, from the expression on Elliot's face, he recognized the apparition. The big gray body with an elongated torso.

Ryleigh, with wide, astonished eyes, backed away from the monster. A large tortoise drifted into her vision, but she never took her eyes off the massive shark following it. Before Elliot and Ryleigh could make a move back to shore, the shark simply flipped his fins and soared... in the other direction. It looked like it was chasing the turtle, but neither one of them stayed around long to watch. She backpedaled into the black tar ripples, retreating to shore, and he followed her. She surfaced, gasped for air, and she floated, rising and falling through the gentle swells carrying her to

146

shore. The beach meant safety – life itself. The night ocean meant death.

He followed her slowly, letting only the salt water carry his weight. Ryleigh was trembling from head to toe with cold and fright. Elliot huddled beside her, and pinched his nose and blew to equalize the pressure he felt on his eardrums. He leaned over and pinched Ryleigh's nose. She half-heartily puckered her lips and swallowed. Elliot wrapped his arms around her as she curled into his lap. She reached out and touched his cheek. Her friend. Her salvation.

"It's okay. We've encountered barracudas and now sharks." Elliot rubbed her shoulders.

It was true. One night under the glare of the flashlight, they had seen a barracuda snatch a midnight snack — a tasty white squid.

"Now what?"

"This is the beauty and the advantage that living on an island offers."

"What, seeing a shark?"

"No, we have plenty of time."

"So we wait? For what?"

"The moon is right, but we can call it a night and go back to camp, or we can try it again."

"Can't we wait until daylight?"

"The tide will make it too deep to explore the reef's crevices. As daylight fades, the lobsters seek refuge under the coral." Elliot always had a scientific answer to her emotional concerns.

"Damn it. You're always right, but I'm okay with eating the flatfish again." She really was sick of the same fish, and her mouth watered when she thought of roasted lobsters.

Maybe it was a test to see what a newly formed couple could endure after a month-long sojourn on a deserted island. Maybe it was the newest moment in a reality show.

How many times had they encountered a life or death situation in the last month?

"Come on. You first!" Elliot said, gesturing toward the reef where the five star restaurant serving fresh lobster tail awaited.

Her fleeting adrenaline rush had been replaced with hunger. Ryleigh dove down again, her eyes groping in relentless gloom. *Come out, come out, wherever you are.*

A myriad of tiny creatures came toward Elliot's light beam. Small schools of frantic fish and prancing shrimp jammed into their glowing beam and made the water flicker with their spasmodic celebrations of light. It was so different than the daylight ocean. At night, the seafloor crawled with life.

When they surfaced for air, Elliot yelled to her, "Ryleigh, get my net and tickle-stick."

Her heart pounded with excitement. The mere thought of real food outweighed anything else. Their time they'd spent Huck Finning around the island had brought them closer.

She handed Elliot the tickle-stick and net. And dove under.

Elliot gave her the loser sign, by placing his thumb and index fingers to his forehead in the shape of an "L". Underwater, it meant they were a winner because he spotted a lobster.

She saw the spiny lobsters with long antennae, surrounding the rocks! There was a small octopus in residence atop another neighboring rock. Scorpion-looking fish loitered on the bottom, confident of their camouflage. The oceanic scene was littered with life, along with the occasional soda or beer can.

Their weekly trysts into the dark sea left them with animated appetizers fit for a king.

Ryleigh waited with the small net. Elliot put the tickle-stick behind their tails, coaxing the lobster, that typically jetted backwards by flexing their tails, to move forward instead, right into Ryleigh's net. The tickle-stick jerked through the cave opening, filled with half a dozen or so lobsters, each the length of a grown man's forearm. One walked forward and Ryleigh trapped it in her net before it could shoot out.

They came up for air. "It's a keeper, "he said.

"They're all keepers." She knew Elliot couldn't control a lot of their troubles, but he could control their diet. In fact, they ate very well. Very healthily. Their weight loss could be attributed to the fact that they'd had very few processed foods. Her normally curvy figure was now lean and sinewy. Everything they ate was fresh – healthy seafood, fruits, plants, and vegetables. She was dying for a greasy hamburger and fries. She truly understood Jimmy Buffet's song, "Cheeseburger in Paradise."

The cheeseburger was soon forgotten as Elliot found a few giant rocks, and looking under them, they found more lobsters than they could actually fit into their net. The lobsters were piled on top of each other. There were so many that they could pick and choose which ones to take.

They filled the net, and Ryleigh kicked and flapped to shore. Elliot stayed behind like he usually did on these reef nights. Just before she touched the sandy beach bottom, she watched her Hunkleberry man spear a good-sized snapper, piercing it behind the gills.

Lying on shore, she examined the contents in the net. Five medium-sized lobsters. The feeling inside her was amazing, champion-like, as though she were a native whose only limitation was the need for food, water, shelter, and air. She was beginning to ignore that feeling of being stranded, that separation from reality. There they sat, a thin veneer dividing one life from the other. Suspended in another world, connected only by the thin hope of rescue.

FORTY

WATCHING RYLEIGH EAT lobster was seductive. She pulled off a leg and sucked out the juice, batting her long lashes at him. She peeled back the shell with captivating vigor.

"What are you staring at? You've seen me eat lobster many times." Ryleigh rolled her tongue over her lips, catching the lingering juices. She carefully lifted the tail meat from the shell, and set the juicy roasted white meat aside.

"I love watching you. You look happy, like we're sitting in a fine restaurant."

"There's not a restaurant in the world that could make this taste any fresher. When we get back home, I'm never wearing a bib to eat lobster again."

"And you shouldn't." Elliot enjoyed the inside body of the lobster – the intestine, the vein, the eggs, the parts Ryleigh didn't like. They ate fish grilled in coconut oil, or fabulous smoked fish and boiled crabs. Elliot did all the cooking, which concerned him.

He had tried to teach her basic food skills and how to start a fire without the grill, but she'd told him, she would always have him there to help her. Deep down, he knew that she would need to learn, even though she had never taken much interest in the campfire business.

She had cooked fish once and served it with mashed breadfruit. It had tasted cold, and different from how he cooked. But she'd served it in the nude, so what could he complain about?

"Elliot, do you think your brother is looking for you yet?" She gently wiped the end of her mouth with the large neck of the black striped t-shirt she was wearing.

"No. We weren't that close."

"But we've been missing for over a month."

"It's not uncommon for me to go on trips and be out-of-pocket for lengths at a time." Guilty feelings were new to Elliot. He was continuing to lie to someone he was starting to have deep feelings for. "What about you, Ryleigh?"

"What about me?"

"I just wanted to know your state of mind. You seem upbeat most of the time."

"My state of mind changes like that goddamn tide out there. Right now, it's not optimistic, but encouraged. As time goes on, I worry, though. I mean, I'm not ready to jump off a cliff, if that's what you're worried about. I'm tired of being stuck here, but being stuck with you has made it better."

"Well, I'm glad to hear that." He worried she couldn't cope alone.

Sitting beside him, Ryleigh kicked at a random sand pile. "Elliot, I care a lot about you. Even though we were forced here accidentally, being here with you has made me really appreciate who you are, and what you mean to me. But why do I feel you're holding back?"

"Ryleigh, there's a small thing I have been keeping from you." Elliot stopped eating and moved closer alongside her.

"I'm all ears."

"When I said I never slept with my ex-girlfriend, after I moved out, well, I did, and I've been lying about it."

There was silence that followed, which was worse than an outburst of surprise or excusing criticism. As they continued to sit by the fire, the pressure to say something, to explain himself, was overbearing.

What was the big deal? Why didn't Ryleigh speak? She was never silent.

He ate a few more bites, then stopped and put one hand on her shoulder, lifting her sulking head with the other, "Ryleigh, it wasn't like that."

"Uh, huh," was all she could dredge up.

"Come on, Ryleigh."

Silence. She kept eating.

Finally, after ten minutes of the silent treatment, she said, "Is it true that the ocean currents flow west of here, always?"

Though Elliot was unsure whether her question was forgiveness or a diversion, he was happy and relieved to explain the ocean's currents. He dove into a colorful explanation of the ocean's currents and how they flowed the opposite from what you'd expect on the Gulf Stream. A dissertation answer that lasted until well after they'd finished their lobsters.

"So when did you sleep with Jeannie?" Ryleigh pulled her knees under her large shirt.

"Ryleigh, it was the holidays. You and I weren't that serious. It was over a year ago."

"But you said you'd never been together again. After you broke up."

"I was there over the holidays, to see her mom, "he said, which wasn't the full truth – he had seen her mom as she'd pulled out of Jeannie's driveway – so it wasn't exactly a lie.

"What else aren't you telling the truth about?"

"Well, honestly, as you can tell, I dye some of my gray hairs now and then." He knew over the last few weeks that he'd seen a few gray hairs popping out here and there on his chin. He was thirty-eight, and it had been the first time for him to see gray in the small mirror hanging in the hut. He hoped to get a chuckle from her, but she turned to him with a serious expression.

"Elliot, that's not what I mean. Like, why are you so fit?" She put up her hand. "And don't say it was high school football. Why do you know so much about survival? Don't say the boy scouts, either."

How could Elliot explain to her what he did? About the agency? Elliot's thoughts went to what he'd done in the past ten years, when he'd been a SEAL. He'd done black ops, been to remote places, and had more than a few scrapes and seen things he never wanted to see again. He was a trained professional, not prone to falling in love, not prone to being reckless in the middle of an adrenaline-full moment... in the middle of an assignment.

"Ry, it's not that simple."

"Elliot, you have to trust me. Who would I tell? We're here alone, and when we get back, your secrets stop at me." She reached down and her petite hand cupped his.

He had submitted to interrogations, truth drugs, and lie detector machines, and passed. But sitting here with Ryleigh, he felt a greater obligation.

"I really am a history teacher, and–"

"–please don't lie. It makes it worse."

"Have you told me everything about your life back home?" Elliot knew she'd purposely left off her past and present's finer details.

Damn her. How could she be so beautiful? She studied his eyes and the tension was thick, but all he wanted to do was pull her into his arms and make love to her.

"Don't make this about me. I asked you first."

"No, I volunteered the information."

"About your ex, yes, and we have talked about that for the last thirteen months. I already knew you had been with her once, but that was before we were even dating steadily. You're always avoiding something in our discussions, and I can't pinpoint it."

Elliot looked into the fire, as if the answers were there. Ryleigh had pushed him to the limits. She really did know him and could read him.

"People we love, we lie to because we worry about them handling the truth, and fear they'll make irrational choices. We lie to them for their own good."

"You mean you don't trust them with the truth." She laid her hand on his thigh. "I'm falling in love with you and I feel you are with me. We have to trust each other."

"I will share in due time. Can we just relax in the aftermath of an amazing dinner, me with an amazing girl who says she loves me?"

"I agree, we can drop it for now." She took the worn thin beach towel off the lawn chair. His heart raced faster and he felt a stirring in his shorts. The beach towel was what Ryleigh lay on to keep the sand chiggers off her when they made love on the beach.

Hard to argue when she stood there seductively urging him to follow her.

"There's something to be said about the ocean and the beach in the moonlight that is calming and romantic." She took his hand and pulled him toward the smooth part of the sloping shore. She spread out the towel and they sat looking out to the water.

"Elliot, right now, right here, it's you and I, and we can forget our past and lives at home. This life is only us." She untied the fraying rope he used as a belt and tugged his shorts off.

She pulled off her t-shirt and swimsuit bottom, and they made love under the stars, then lay wrapped in each other's arms with the glow of the moon on the majestic sea, making anything else he could say now sound pathetic. The island with its secrets seemed enchanted. Did Ryleigh know him well? Or was he succumbing to the moonlight's charms and finally picturing himself falling in love with Ryleigh? What would he be like as a husband…. calm, serious, unmovable Elliot?

Elliot had never told her that he loved her, and she'd never wondered until now if he did. They were both so busy with their separate lives that, when they were together, it was always about great sex.

It was true he'd never felt that with anyone.

Ryleigh sat up on her elbows and ran her fingers up and down his arm. She didn't say much and neither did Elliot.

She puckered her full lips in a kiss and blew it at him.

"Let's go to the hut. The wild animals at night are scary."

"How about we go to the hut and make wild animal noises and scare the animals?"

"Race you." Her gorgeous nude body took off across the sand toward the hut.

Elliot loved how Ryleigh enjoyed the escapes to fantasy – because he could never fall in love with someone that was entirely grounded in reality. He felt the connection, and closer now to her than he'd ever felt before. His lying wasn't to keep the peace in their relationship: it was for protection, and to preserve a sense of safety from a force out of his control.

FORTY-ONE
Texas

THE THIRD FLOOR of the apartment complex smelled worse than the first floor. Chandler had ascended the staircase almost positive that he'd find a decaying animal in it, but to his surprise, when he got to Candy's apartment, he found the young girl's place tidy.

So far, the interview had been cordial and colorful. She'd willingly answered questions. Not a normal street girl. She looked to be twenty-one, and maybe life on the streets hadn't toughened her up yet.

"Candy, did your girlfriend know anyone else on the boat?" Chandler asked.

She opened her mouth. Shut it. Shook her head. "No, but Arrie may have borrowed those clothes she had on, and maybe that's how she ended up with 'em."

"Now who's playing detective?"

The girl giggled, and took a cigarette and a lighter from the coffee table. Before the cigarette was lit, a Hispanic man of about forty poked his head in the door and asked her to come downstairs for a second.

"Eat shit and die." She yelled after him. "He's a little possessive and doesn't like men up here who he doesn't know."

"Tell him I have a badge. That will keep him away."

"Santos, this guy's a cop, from the cruise ship. Said he'll arrest your ass if you don't leave us alone." She took a long pull on the cigarette.

The door slammed and the apartment went quiet.

"So you think she 'borrowed' the passenger's shorts?" Chandler seemed uninterested, but he really only had a few minutes. He was anxious to catch a plane back to Tampa, and traffic in South Houston had been horrendous.

The girl didn't answer. She shrugged and said, "I did see her pick up some random clothes on the beach."

"The beach? Not the ship?"

"Yeah, the party beach."

"Okay, that's helpful." That would explain the age differences of the two vics and the mixed identities. Leave it to the Port Authority and Transportation Department to screw it up.

"Look, she's dead, and ya'all are just now coming to talk to me."

"Didn't they already question you?"

"Yes, after the accident, at port. But no one here in the U.S."

"I'm working for the insurance side. And these kinds of investigations take time, especially for accidents."

"I understand." She blew out a long stream of smoke. "Actually, I've been hard to get ahold of. Stayed on an extended vacay, with the reimbursement the cruise line gave me."

Thoughtfully, she smiled at him. Chandler had observed that in some of his victims he interviewed – a guilty pleasure in the surrendering of secrets. He wasn't their analyst, or therapist, or confessor, but the more they talked, he knew the more relaxed they got, and the more they babbled information. Usually not helpful to his case, but occasionally he found a clue of evidence he'd missed.

"I went to Australia for a few weeks. Imagine that. Me, down under. L.O.L." She actually appeared to want to be cross-questioned by him about her trip, about how she'd paid for it. And was she flirting with him?

He was a lot older than her, and felt no connection. Probably in her profession, she automatically batted her eyelashes at all the men she talked to.

Chandler continued to interrogate her about her trip, but she didn't divulge anything that would be helpful to the investigation. He needed to reel the conversation back in to the cruise.

"Does your roomie have a family?"

"She's not my roomie. She only crashed here occasionally. Santos paid both of us to work the cruise ship. Those horny college guys are a sure bet. And most of the time, they pass out or throw up before even getting their pants down."

"Easy money?"

"Yeah, I guess you could say that."

"Who can I talk to about the girl that went on the cruise with you and Santos?"

"The guy you just scared out of the apartment building."

"Figures." There went his chance to catch the last flight to Florida. He pulled out a card and gave it to her. It had one word on it and a telephone number. "If you think of anything else or Santos comes back soon, call this number. It's my private cell. Sorry for your loss."

She studied the card and got all sad-looking. "I was so busy when we got back. I had to take her clients, too, you know. Now that it's sinking in, do you think the cruise company will pay for her insurance, or some sort of bereavement?"

"You'll have to call them and sort it out." He walked toward the door and opened it, but before he left, he said, "Call me if you have any other thoughts about the shorts and who they belonged to. And call your parents; I'm sure they'd love to hear you're safe."

He shut the door and held his breath as he descended down the putrid stairwell.

FORTY-TWO
Keg Key

RYLEIGH FLOATED on the inner tube, her number one favorite pastime. She had read the paperback she'd found in the hut six times already. Today, she was content to bird and dolphin watch.

Hunk Finn Elliot was out exploring. Alone. Again. When he returned, they were to have a long-needed talk. He had told her when they were on the flower hillside several days ago that he wanted to discuss something with her. Answers she wanted to know. About him. About them.

The little birds she called the 'swallows of the sea' pitter-pattered on top of the ocean's surface, feeding. A pelican made a nose dive, plunging into the water and pulling out a fish, and she watched other birds that no land dweller would ever see, because these pelagic birds spent their lives at sea. If she caught enough birds, could she pluck them and make a skirt of colorful feathers?

She waited for the pod of dolphins that played and circled her often. She and Elliot had jumped in with them a few times and mimicked what they did. They would get bored and take off, and later return, clicking and chattering away.

There really was so much to enjoy while she was afloat. But today it wasn't enjoyable. She drifted with her feet dangling in the water, soon to have ten shriveled-up prune toes.

She had been waiting for their rescue boat for over four weeks, and she prayed it came soon, because she was gonzo with boredom.

She grabbed her tube of sunscreen and took a pea size squirt, and rubbed it under her eyes.

"Screw it." She took off the cap again, and this time she squeezed the tube until her cupped hand was full of the greasy, white lotion. She rubbed it on her arms, bare chest, and stomach, but she let it sit on her skin. This time, she didn't rub it in. After she finished using the entire tube of SPF 55, she tossed the empty, orange bottle into the sea. She watched as it floated for a few minutes, filled with water, and sank to the seafloor just four feet below her.

Her life had gone to hell in a hand basket over the last year or so, ever since she'd stumbled on the Dexco clinical trial results. The real results. It wasn't her fault, and her hiding from it was not right. That's why she'd agreed to testify in the class action suit. *Who wouldn't?* It's not fair she felt the way she did, but life too often wasn't fair either. She knew the possible consequences. *Get fired from Dexco, or worse, get threatened. Chased. Hunted.*

Guilty feelings, about her frivolously over-using the tiki hut supplies and then littering their pristine world, made her feel restless.

She tried to retrieve the empty tube of lotion, but her raft kept drifting away, and the orange subject of her attention seemed to be darting off in the opposite direction. She paddled a little farther, but gave up for the time being.

She thought of Caleigh, her sister, and what she might be feeling. Since Ryleigh had left her a half desperate voice message four weeks ago, surely Caleigh was looking for her. Somebody had to be. Even Dexco executives, as anxious as they were to get rid of her, had to be filling her position and wondering why she'd left without giving notice. Did anyone care that she was missing? Did anyone wonder why Elliot hadn't checked in? Maybe his ex-girlfriend was worried.

She stared at the water. When everything in her life was uncertain, shouldn't her relationship with him have been quite clear by now? *Elliot, Hunk-a-berry, who are you, my love?*

Her unsettled state of mind was compounded by the discussion they were to have in a few hours.

She dove off the raft and searched for the spent tube of sunscreen. Her eyes stung in the saltwater. She stepped on it and brought it up from the bottom of the ocean floor.

She closed her stinging eyes and tried to imagine life back home with him. She had tears all over her face, but it didn't feel like crying in the water. The salt on her face from the ocean mixed with the salt of her tears.

This sand- covered beach was more familiar to her than the man she slept with every night. She knew him, and that was the problem: she knew he was hiding something and today he would tell her when he returned. She would make him tell her everything.

Ryleigh had settled on the lawn chair nearest the hut after changing to dry clothes. Another t-shirt. She wondered if she would ever wear the same one twice before they were rescued. She stared frequently at the forest trail openings for the rest of the afternoon.

Elliot had said they "would talk," but where was he? He'd said today he would tell her. He had never taken this long before when he'd left for the day. She could hear the slop, slop, slop of the waves against the tiki hut's pilings. A deep chill shivered up her spine, and intuition overcame her.

"Elliot? Elliot? Are you in the hut? Where are you?"

No answer. The beach was as silent as a painting.

Her worries about their talk were now replaced, dread taken over with genuine fear. She trembled, but Ryleigh didn't know if his tardy return was a premonition.

Here they were, stranded together and bound by nature and survival. She loved him. Or was it a convenience since he was the only other person in her life? Love was never convenient.

He still hadn't returned at early dusk when she sat in the tiki hut on the hard bedroll, debating if she should go look for him. She wanted to leave the beach, but he had made her promise a few days ago that if he was ever detained or late, that she would wait patiently before roaming the island.

So she would wait. But for how long?

FORTY-THREE

RYLEIGH LAY there for hours, until day evaporated to night. She heard unusual sounds outside the hut. "Elliot, is that you? Come in, will you?"

Shit, no response. She took the small fileting knife that one of the cooks had left behind. Elliot always carried the large knife. She held it tight, exited the hut, and gazed into the dark night in stark terror.

This was her first time to be alone on the island at night. Her scalp, neck, and back prickled, leaving her tiny hairs standing on end.

"I have to go find Elliot," she said, looking at the empty tiki hut. And then she said, "hold down the fort," a saying Elliot had told her before he went exploring.

She lit a bamboo torch that Elliot had made with rags and oils. "Hunkleberry, I'll find you," her voice whispered out, choked in fear. Elliot had the only flashlight.

She held the knife in one hand and the dim torch in the other. She started out on the path to the cave where Elliot had her hide when the pirates attacked.

Each step crackled, and suddenly a bird squawked and darted out. Stumbling in panic, she dropped the knife.

"Elliot! Elliot! Damn it, where are you?" She felt an incongruous twinge of helplessness. Tears streamed down her face. She searched with only the skimpy guidance of the torch on the dark path, grabbing the knife and tucking it into the waistband of her bikini bottom that now had lost half its rhinestones. She covered the back of the knife with her white short-sleeve t-shirt with a large sailor wheel on the front. *Dear Lord, please let him be okay.*

She felt a scratch on her knee. "Damn." She pulled on the scraped skin, and fresh drops of blood appeared and rolled down her leg. She took a deep breath, wiped her tears with the back of her hand, and in a more composed and determined manner, she quickened her stride. *I'll find you, Elliot, hang tight.*

She made her way slowly to the cave, aware that she'd forgotten to apply bug spray because of the immense number of mosquitos attacking her legs, ankles, arms, and face.

Mercifully, she saw the cave ahead, and she let out a long-held breath. She squirmed, knowing in her heart of hearts that Elliot wasn't there.

"Elliot. Are you there, babe?" Her voice was hoarse and foreign-sounding.

She felt something rub against her neck.

"EWW!" She jumped and spun around in circles, knife in one hand, torch in the other. "Get off of me! Get off of me!" She waved her knife-bearing hand over her shoulder.

Satisfied the spider was no longer crawling on her neck, she pushed away the brush and crawled on all fours toward the cave's dark opening, careful to inspect each movement she made, before putting her hand down. Her cut knee stung.

Oh God, I hope he's here.

The entrance to the cave was stuffy, and gray. Not completely dark. But there was no movement. If Elliot was inside, he wasn't moving. "Elliot, baby, are you there?" As she progressed, she sensed recent animal or human presence, mildew, and urine – her fear escalated. The inside of the cave came into focus.

Crawling partially into the cave, she felt something slither over her bent-back calf. *Hell no. Hell-the-fuck-no!* Her inner mind screamed, but she wouldn't breathe, or move. She was as still as the musty cave air. The slithering continued across her legs and

165

she quickly figured it had to be at least an eight foot snake. *No! Not another snakebite!* Her healed wrist throbbed.

Once she felt it clear her leg, she slowly reached for the knife she had deposited back in her waistband. That's when she heard the hissing. The monstrous snake was a few inches from her head. For an instant, just an instant, complete, mindless panic struck.

She screamed and frantically tried to stab the snake with little to no success. Uncontrollable gasps escaped from her throat as she violently stabbed the ground and air around her, waving the torch's slightly lit flames. She felt the knife hit something soft, and she thought it was the reptile. Scrunching her eyes, she tried to see what her knife was stuck in. With her free hand, she moved the dim light to her knife.

For a fleeting moment, the snakes forgotten and Elliot's disappearance on hold, she saw a brown leather billfold, stuck to her blade.

She felt the smooth calfskin between her fingers. Excitement pounded in her heart. She hid it between the rolls of her t-shirt sleeve, like a pack of cigarettes, and backed quickly and noisily out of the cave.

Then she ran. Instinct again driving her back down the path toward camp. "Elliot, I can't find you, babe. You're not in the cave. Where are you?!" She gasped at the top of her lungs.

Birds scattered everywhere, and her voice echoed out in the open and behind her.

A dark shadow moved on the path coming from the hut. "Now what? Oh God, now what?" Her words were breathless, and she felt the urge to wet her bikini bottoms.

"Ryleigh," Elliot yelled.

"Oh my God, Elliot." She ran down the path, not caring where she stepped in the process. She jumped into his arms.

"Ryleigh, what are you doing out here? You could have been hurt." He smoothed his hands over her hair.

"I was looking for you. Where were you?"

Elliot hesitated, "You were searching for me? Out here? I can't believe you'd risk your life for me."

"Of course. I'm a bloody idiot, but I love you, Elliot, and I wasn't going to sit around while you were out here in danger. Where were you?"

"I slipped on one of the cliffs on the west side, while exploring one of the caves, and it got late and high tide came in, quicker than I thought, stranding me there, waiting for the water to reside–"

"– just kiss me, Elliot." She pressed her lips to his and her hands held both of his rough, stubbly cheeks. "If you ever leave like that again, I'll kill you." And to emphasize her comment, she pulled out the small knife.

"Ryleigh, you astound me."

"When did you get back to the hut?"

"I've been back at the camp for about thirty minutes. As soon as I found out you were gone, I went searching. You scared the hell out of me, too, young lady."

They walked back to the hut hand-in-hand. The breeze brought a sudden relief, and Ryleigh shivered, conscious of the thin wallet wrapped in her shirt sleeve.

For a fleeting moment, she almost told Elliot, but something kept her silent. A feeling inside. A treasure she wanted to explore alone.

FORTY-FOUR

THE FOLLOWING DAY. Elliot was glad to see Ryleigh sleeping in because they were both exhausted after their adventures the night before.

They slept shoulder-to-shoulder in the hut every night, awakened occasionally by a passing squall, but last night they had both collapsed in each other's arms and a 727 couldn't have woken them.

He had been up early and he now prepared a hefty breakfast. Both had been ravished when they'd gone to bed.

He mostly cooked with ingredients left behind in the hut, and what they gathered from the island. Coconuts had become a better staple than Crisco. It was a great source of milk and oil, and coconut meat shaved and sprinkled on berries made a sweet dessert; Ryleigh used softened, mushy coconut squeezed and kneaded through a t-shirt to make lotions for her skin, and they even used it for brushing their teeth... and it made great fish bait.

The sun would be blazing through the burlap hut windows, and he knew Ryleigh would be up soon.

He stirred the mashed breadfruit and poured the coconut milk on the berries, thinking about the tough talk they would have today.

"Good morning." Ryleigh walked out of the hut wearing a white t-shirt with tropical flowers on the front and her golden tan peaks shoving through the thin material. She looked glorious, as usual. She strode over to him, her bright green eyes assessing him and the breakfast shrewdly. She surprised him by not kissing him good morning, but he chalked it up to exhaustion.

"Good morning, my crazy, brave girl." His voice didn't waver because, in his heart, he was filled with gratitude and compassion for what she'd done last night, especially having to kill the eight foot snake she'd told him about while they'd laid in each other's arms. She'd even bent the tip of the small knife, stabbing it.

She didn't respond. She squeezed his hand, but remained mute, and her usual cheerful brow rippled like a Ruffle potato chip.

"How are you feeling today?" He stirred the breadfruit and pulled the metal bowl off the open fire, using a t-shirt as an oven mitt.

"I've felt better. I'm sore." She eyed him, and her expression was like that of a hunted predator, with all her senses alerted.

"Are you hungry?"

"Always."

"I'm famished, too. Come sit." He pulled out their favorite luminous yellow, woven lawn chairs with wood armrests that Ryleigh swore were made out of eucalyptus because they smelled great.

He handed her a cardboard box lid that they used as a plate, filled with a generous amount of food; grilled fish, mashed breadfruit, berries, all pleasantly arranged, no matter how primal it was. Ryleigh drank from a souvenir mug full of warm coconut milk, her de facto island cup of joe.

"I thought you were famished?" Elliot asked as he watched Ryleigh push her food around.

"I guess I'm not as hungry as I thought."

He did a quick calculation, worried that it was her time of the month again, but it wasn't. Something was seriously bothering her, and he knew it was time to talk.

He took her makeshift plate away and sat next to her. "Ryleigh, I know you think you want a bunch of answers, to things I can't share…"

"Can't or won't?"

"Both."

"Why? What makes you so special?"

"I'm not special. I just have secrets that are better left undiscovered. Not yet anyway. There are some things that I have lied about, yes, but it was for your protection."

"Maybe start with who Elliot Finn really is?"

He frowned. "Ryleigh, you know who I am," he said quietly, clearly concerned about her reason for asking. *What does she know? Where is this going?*

"You're not a history teacher, are you?"

"Why do you question that?"

"You're too survival - talented, to be a teacher, especially a history teacher."

"I'll take that as a compliment somewhere in there."

"Why do you have this?" Ryleigh pulled a billfold from the back of her bottoms, opening it to produce a tarnished badge with his name on it.

"Where did you find that?"

"Never mind that. Why are you lying? Can we finally talk? I mean, really talk?"

Elliot rubbed his hands over his face. He'd known this was coming, he'd known this shoe would drop some day, but he'd hoped not until the game was played out. So maybe, in a horrible way, it was better to get it done. Now he knew why she was giving him the cold shoulder. He left it in the cave. *What else did she find there?*

Agreeing to her last request... maybe it is time to really talk.

"I have a confession to make; I've been keeping a secret from you for a year or so. Since we met." He needed to give her some answers.

"I knew it." She stood up.

"Hear me out. I'm telling this to you now, not because I have to, but because I care deeply about you and I have a plan to make it right." He did have a plan, but how delicate should he be with her? Ryleigh was smart, and he shouldn't sugarcoat it.

"I see. I'll be the judge."

He still was who he was, no matter what client had hired him. No matter who the victim was that his client had hired him to pursue.

With the muscles in his shoulders clenching like fists, he took a deep breath and said, "Dexco hired me to watch you."

Elliot had waited half a dozen months to tell her, but now, telling her, he had a huge lump in his throat as he threw those six words at her.

Ryleigh brought her hand over her mouth, her eyes reflecting fear and dismay. Before Elliot could say another word, she threw the coffee cup down, shattering it, and she ran toward the beach.

FORTY-FIVE

ELLIOT CHASED Ryleigh to the end of the beach by the rocks. As he chased her, he considered lying to her again, not just to shield her from worry, but because he didn't want to get her killed, or to waste time in explanations of his past. But lying to her had become harder and harder, so he decided to go for the partial truth.

"Hey, come on, babe. It's not what you're thinking." He arched a brow, not sure how she would feel about him.

She held her hands to her head. Her emerald eyes locked on his. "Are you serious? Who are you?"

For seconds, he didn't reply. Finally, he leaned over to her and put his hand around her shoulder. She pushed it off.

"Elliot." She stared at him blankly, her eyes filling with tears. She rubbed her temples.

He tried again to come toward her.

She stepped back, and held up her hand, "Don't you touch me!" She spread her hands open with fingers apart like she was protecting herself from him.

It killed him to see her hurt over the truth – and the partial truth, at best.

"So our whole relationship is a lie?" Tears streamed down her face.

"No, Ryleigh, not all of it."

"What then? Who hired you to screw me for a year, to wine and dine me, then strand me here, and then what were you to do? Kill me? Or leave me here to die?" Her voice cracked, but she maintained her business-like composure. Sweet Ryleigh, always trying to maintain control.

"I wasn't going to kill you, ever." He spoke sincerely, but in his mind, the lies were evident, and he wondered if she'd ever believe a word he said. Ryleigh looked so shocked and openly scared that she wouldn't recognize the truth if she heard it, or not.

He continued to try and convince her. "Surveillance isn't always about watching someone. It's about relationships, too. So getting to know you and have you in my life was planned – yes. But then it turned to something more."

She turned and started walking quickly down the beach. Elliot followed her. The beach trail beaten flat from their bare feet stretched from the rocks to the hut.

"Ryleigh, I didn't mean to hurt you. I was keeping you out of the way." It was true, that he had planned to get to know her, and her habits, and have her trust him enough to take her away with him. He'd never intended to fall in love with her. It was supposed to be an easy assignment. He'd never gotten a conscience on assignments; with her, it had been different from the beginning.

"You didn't plan to strand us? Is this why life here hasn't been a Tom Hanks-*Castaway* nightmare? You stocked this island for us to hide out? Correct?"

"Slow down. I did plan some things. I could never have planned that storm. That was coincidental."

"Lucky you. Maybe they'll pay you a bonus for the storm tidying up everything." She had backed further away from him. She was on the threshold of the beach, near the rocks.

"Can we sit down and talk?"

"Why? To add insult to injury, you're going to tell me that you enjoyed getting to know me, and now…"

Tears rolled down her cheeks. She wiped her hand to her eyes, and sniffled.

"The important thing is that we're here together and I can help you."

"Minor details, really? Really, Elliot!" She took her fists and pounded on his chest.

He grabbed her wrists and pulled her to his face. "Please, Ryleigh, we need to talk about this. You weren't so honest yourself. You didn't trust me, did you?"

She pushed back and looked at him. "You're right. I didn't want to share my issues at Dexco with you. It's a white lie. It's not something you bring up in a new relationship. Not yet. 'Hey, let's go on a cruise together because I'm being watched by my company.' It's in-your-face drama."

"I would have listened."

"Of course, you're on their side."

"I'm not on their side."

"You're their hired assassin."

"For the record, I'm not an assassin. I'm a special agent, turned P.I."

"Okay, then who are you, really? Is your name even Elliot?" She questioned him with shock and revulsion.

"Ryleigh, sit. Please sit down." He directed her toward a flat rock on the edge of the beach. He brushed the crushed shells, and planted her down. He took a seat on another rock with his back to the sea. They sat in silence for a few minutes.

She crossed her arms and stared at him. "Talk. Who do you work for?"

Elliot looked at her, two Jacuzzis for eyes. No smile. Heated stare.

"This whole operation was funded by someone in one of the government agencies. Probably a branch of the FDA. The Food and Drug Administration has a lot to do with drug approvals."

"So am I the 'operation'? Please tell me the agency paying you has better things to do than hire a babysitter for me."

174

"Ryleigh, I was in Counter Intelligence and someone burned me."

"Well, that explains a lot of things. The way you have MacGyver-like skills. But the CIA? And how did you get burned?"

"I was outed. You don't need to know the details, but I was stripped of everything. I couldn't write a parking ticket. I was told by the agency that unless I did their dirty work, someone I was close to would be eliminated."

"Killed? Who?"

"Several of my close covert operatives were murdered."

Ryleigh gasped and covered her mouth. "I'm sorry for your loss. But I still don't see, 'why me'?"

"They have someone close to me. They not only got to him, but his family. There are young kids involved. They did this to an innocent family because they want me to do a few jobs. Believe me, Ryleigh, I'd rather have broken a dozen men out of Guantanamo Bay than to take this job."

"Elliot, I know you feel like you have to protect everyone, but it's blackmail, not to mention a few other illegalities. You don't need to solve everything. You could have just walked away."

"I got an innocent man and his family on the hook. If I didn't get close to the sources and work for the agency, they would have hired someone else to do it. And you, me, and that man and his family would all be missing." He stared at a yellow crab, then nudged it with his toe until it fell into a hole in the sand. He prayed she believed it; at least some of it really was the truth.

When she didn't respond, he finally said, "I have a plan."

"Why should I believe you? You've lied a lot. A long list." He didn't think she would believe anything he said right now if his tongue was notarized.

"Yes, and I apologized. But most spies lack that characteristic called honesty. If I didn't follow along, they could have me erased. I can give the agency what they want and nothing more, until I figure this all out."

Ryleigh backed off the rock. "So why haven't you killed me yet?"

He didn't try to stop her when she leaned over him and grabbed his knife, tucked in his shorts.

"They wanted you missing, not dead."

Now what did she think she would do with his knife? Yes, his knife; he hadn't found it in the backpack behind the hut, like he'd told Ryleigh. He'd had it planted there.

"Well, that's comforting." She showed him the knife.

He didn't move, and he nodded, acknowledging her control over the weapon.

"Babe, they wanted you gone for good, but I helped save you from that. I told them, let me get inside her head, her townhouse–"

"–my pants."

"To find out what you know. That you were more valuable to them now, than to be disposed of."

She lifted up the knife with one shaking hand, then used the other hand to steady the knife. Both hands held it above him, as he sat calmly, his eyes pleading with her.

"Have you ever imagined what this day would be like? When were you going to tell me? Or were you ever?"

"I said I had a plan. What was I to do? Just take you on a cruise and say, 'Hi, I'm Elliot, I destroyed your life and stranded you on a remote, deserted island, while lying to you about everything.'"

"Really, Elliot!"

"Ry, listen to my plan, then decide if you want to stab me." His eyes blared at her, hoping his challenge was accepted from his stare.

She lowered the knife.

"Good, that's a start," Elliot said. "Now sit." Taking her hand, he pulled her down beside him.

And for once, she didn't object.

FORTY-SIX

"OKAY, YOU have all my attention." Ryleigh was surprised that her voice sounded so calm, although inside she felt like a mess of emotions.

Elliot gazed at her impassively for a few seconds, and looked at the knife she still held with one hand, it now resting in her lap. She felt betrayed, hurt, and bewildered over everything she had heard this morning. Her head was throbbing and she felt nauseous. Her naked emotions were out in the open; clearly, he could see the expression on her face.

"I don't have to go over the reasons they are concerned about you, do I?"

"Humor me."

"You found documents... wait... correction, you kept private, hidden documents."

"That's my job. I safeguard Dexco documents. I'm a Quality Control Manager, and that's part of QA, safeguarding everything." She wasn't sure he knew what QA stood for, so she clarified. "That's 'Quality Assurance' for you CIA types, that don't know pharmaceutical lingo."

"Are you mocking me?" Elliot arched his eyebrows, illuminating his bluish eyes. The turquoise sea in the background paled in comparison.

Damn, even though she hated him at this very moment, he was still beautiful, so god damn hunk-a-berry.

"I was only doing my job. That's what this is all about. I go through hundreds and hundreds of documents. And Christ, I have to find one, one that catches my eye."

"So you read it?" he frowned.

"Elliot, you know why you're here. I didn't just read it, I investigated it."

"Why, Ryleigh? Haven't you ever heard the saying, 'curiosity killed the cat'?"

She snapped at him. "It was my job! And there were lives at stake. Do you know how many men, women, and children take that drug?" She paused. "Children, Elliot."

Despite her fear and anger with him from moments earlier, she still felt he had a control over her, and she wanted his approval. She blushed. "You would do the same."

"You're probably right. And how were you to know about the investors and the lawsuit?"

"Precisely. I didn't. And still don't know the details."

"At this moment, they're involved in the class action lawsuit that should be over in a few days. Without you there to say anything, Dexco will win. And some celebrated hedge fund healthcare group will put another 600 million into Dexco. All because of that drug."

"God. Then they'll expand, and every doctor and hospital will be using it. It's bad, it kills, and they know it."

"And they know, you know it, too."

"Why would the FDA keep me away? Isn't that the agency that hired you?"

"The FDA has people that are involved, too. They know that companies, like Dexco, tend to overemphasize the good and ignore the bad in their trials."

She loosened the grip on the knife. "So what's the plan?" It was time for her to start thinking beyond the present, and to deal with her future.

"First, you need to tell me everything you know and where you hid the e-documents–"

"–why do I have the sudden feeling you're trying to interrogate me, rather than have a real discussion? How do I know you're not still lying, and that your plan isn't to help me, and not to expose Dexco?"

"Ryleigh, after all we've been through, you still think I'm on their side? How many times have I saved you?" He whispered conspiratorially. Ryleigh's eyes met his. *Did she trust him?* That's what this all boiled down to – their trust in one another.

"Yes, you have saved me." More than he would ever know. "Maybe you're doing it to save yourself."

"I risked my own life for you, and I would again. I saved you from the shark. I cared for you when you were delirious from the coconut cut on your head, saved you from the pirate attack, the snake bite, saved you from starving–"

She raised her eyebrows at him because she wouldn't have starved, and he knew that.

"Ry, you wouldn't have eaten raw fish. You didn't know how to catch, filet, and cook it. You couldn't make a fire without the grill," he said, as he read her mind. "I gave you warm meals, and companionship in the first place. Sooner or later, you have to realize I did all this for you. Without me there to fend off the pirates, you'd still be hiding in that cave."

"The pirates? You didn't scare them off, or indirectly, I guess you did, with the snakes."

"I did get them away, and if we're on to the truth, they weren't exactly pirates," he said, sucking in his lower lip.

"What?" *When will his lies stop?*

"They were sent by the Dexco thugs," Elliot said.

"But you said you recognized that they were pirates. How do you know they were sent here?"

"It was planned, Ryleigh," he said softly. "Those weren't pirate ships; those were ships sent by Dexco. They came here to make sure you were dead. Dexco not only wanted you missing, they wanted proof you wouldn't come back. They wanted me to go back with them and I said no, that I wanted nothing to do with them anymore."

Ryleigh couldn't believe what he was saying. The knife slid from her hands and fell to the wet, hard sand. A crystal clear wave swept over it and the silver blade glistened through the water from the bright sun.

"Was anything on this island real? Or was everything a lie?"

He moved close to her and his arm reached out.

She slid off the rock and whirled around. "Don't touch me," she snapped, and he froze.

"Ryleigh, stop it. I care... can we get past this and move forward... we have a lot to do if we're to make this work...." He gaped at her and had the gall to even look like he was the victim here. His eyes look wounded. Poor Hunk-le-berry, he actually looked in distress.

Well, he should. If she wasn't willing to follow his *plan*, then what would happen to her? She had to go through with it either way, or be left for dead? And then there was one huge problem: she had fallen in love with him.

"Please, Ryleigh," he begged so softly that she wondered if he was speaking aloud. "Please, don't be pissed or frightened of me. I'm still me. I still care for you."

She didn't answer. He continued, "I had a mission, and it didn't include falling in love with you. I have strict rules of conduct and I'm afraid I've broken many rules."

She began to relax, from the calm look in his eyes and the strength of his arm as he wrapped it around her waist. She felt the protectiveness of his non-threatening stance, and the warmth and scent of his body to guide her. She exhaled. Were all the cards on the table?

FORTY-SEVEN

RYLEIGH GAZED out at the beautiful panoramic sea and, without looking at Elliot, she said, "I'm not saying yes yet, to the plan. But I'm open. Let's start from the beginning."

Elliot sighed and ran a hand through his hair. "I've told you the beginning. First a Counter Intelligence Agent. "

"You're what? CIA?"

"Ex-Seal turned CIA turned P.I."

"Navy Seal? That explains the swimming and a lot of other things. Are you even a professor? Or was that all a lie?"

Elliot sat back and cupped his hands around the back of this head.

"Are you a P.I. or hit man?"

"Yes, I've had to kill a few people. I'm not proud of that, but it was for our country. Not a hit man." Elliot spent the next twenty minutes explaining to her his formal military training background.

"Oh God, Elliot. Where does this leave me? Us? Catch me up to date. What happened that day with the two speed boats?"

"The cruisers? The pirates?"

"Yes. They didn't come to shore because they were waiting for a signal from you?" All of sudden, that day was making sense to her. "What did they want?"

"They wanted your body, and I don't mean alive."

She couldn't contain her fury. "Fuck, Elliot. Are you serious?" Was he trying to frighten her? "And what did you tell them? Did you see them?" She muttered, breathing heavily, deliberating, and trying to stay calmer than she felt.

"I did see them. I lied, twisted the story I told to you when I got you from the cave." He paused and watched her eyes.

"Keep going," she said, thinking this couldn't get any worse.

"I only told you parts of that day. When I came to the camp, the captain was waiting for me and wanted to see where your body was buried. I gave him the t-shirts."

"The t-shirts?" She blinked at him and then narrowed her eyes, urging him to continue.

"The bloody shirts. I told them you'd been attacked by a shark and bled out."

"But how? Won't they see it wasn't my blood? Was it the boar you killed in the woods? They're a pharmaceutical company; they could have done a blood test before they left the cove."

"And they probably did. "

She was still, staring but not blinking, dumfounded, dazed – a massive tide smashing, wave by wave, through her heart.

"Ryleigh, it was your blood. I used the t-shirts I strategically gave you during that time you gashed your leg open on the coral–"

"–Elliot, that's not enough blood–"she said, hiding the swirl of confusion she had inside. But now it made sense, that he had folded them just so. The tiny white shirts.

"I'm so sorry, Ryleigh.

"What?" *No. No. No.* She remembered how, after the cut from the coral, he had stayed up all night nursing her, cleaning the wound. All the time, draining her blood carefully on the clean shirts.

"Oh my God, Elliot." Tears pricked in the corner of her eyes and a large lump got stuck in her throat.

He shook his head slowly.

She covered her mouth with her hand while tears slid down her cheeks. She lowered her head and finally let herself go. Sobbing. Heaving unladylike sighs of loss and relief.

FORTY-EIGHT

RYLEIGH EYED the knife lying on the sand; every few waves, its blade was washed with the salty sea water. She swallowed hard. She had never used a gun or a knife on a person and she wasn't about to try against her CIA-hunk-Finn. But he didn't know that.

She wiped the tears from her face and hopped down off the rock. She took a deep breath and, in a more composed but hurt manner, she bent down and grabbed the knife, and strode toward the hut.

"Ryleigh, wait up. Don't you want to finish?"

"What's the point? Everyone already thinks I'm dead back home, right?" She yelled over her shoulder.

Elliot caught up to her and tried to grab her hand. She pulled it away. "Please, Ryleigh." He looked mortified.

She quickened her stride. "How?" She slowed her pace to look at him as they walked back to the hut. "How could my blood be enough? And, who knows? Just Dexco?"

"If you let me finish, "he inhaled, "I'll explain it all." His voice was a breathless echo across the beach. "They're a tough group to be involved with, and unless they believe that I'm all the way in and I mean business, then we could both be dead. They need to know that I'm someone that they can take seriously."

"You have a very interesting way of showing them I'm dead."

"They have more than your blood."

Even with her face bright red from crying and the constant sunburn, she felt herself pale. "How?"

"I have ways. I have access to records, dental...." He trailed off and stopped when they reached the yellow lawn chairs.

"Sit."

Ryleigh plunked down, side-saddle on the lounge chair.

"I wanted to make sure, they'd take me seriously."

"You're a green beret; you could kill me with your little finger..."

"...a SEAL, not a beret."

"But how did you fake them?"

"I knew before we got here. I had some teeth, in the cave–"

"–Mine?" She'd had dental surgery last year, but how would Elliott know her dentist, Garry?

He didn't answer her and kept talking. "I told them after I started the deed, you ran from me, bleeding, to the water, and, well, sharks did the rest."

Ryleigh glared at Elliot, gaping at him in horror. She thought of her sister and wondered if she knew. And thank God her parents weren't alive to learn that one of their twin daughters had been eaten by sharks on a cruise.

Elliot grabbed her by the forearms and pulled her face to his. "Ryleigh, we have to do this together for it to work. If we decide we need a little insurance, then what do you have on them? What exactly did you find?"

Ryleigh stared into his eyes. Her Huckleberry Finn. Her lover, boyfriend, companion, her only other human being she had even talked to in the last six weeks. She couldn't answer. She just stared back.

"Ry, if I brought you back to testify, then they will most likely make you and me disappear permanently. I care too much for you to let that happen."

She groaned. When he said things like that, her heart swelled with love, and when that happened, it didn't seem to matter that Elliot was who he'd said he was.

"What exactly do you have in mind? Did it ever occur to you that they would eventually take this babysitting to the next level?"

The knife suddenly felt heavy and ridiculous in her hand, but she couldn't put it down.

"Look, Ryleigh, I'm not a saint. I've done a lot of terrible things. But I'm running out of time. They have a dear person of mine and that made a shift in circumstances."

"Who? Who is it that you would make a deal with the devil for?"

A halting frown crossed Elliott's face. In it, she didn't see some coldblooded kidnapper, just her guy who had saved her all these weeks. Just her guy that had gone too far and dug himself in too deep. Even so, she held onto the knife.

"My brother, Ryleigh, my older brother," he paused and his eyes were glassy, "and my two nieces, Emily who's five and Sarah, seven."

"Oh my God, Elliot. I'm so sorry." She thought of her sister and knew she'd do anything for Caleigh, her flesh and blood. She didn't know what to do. She reached out and let her free hand gently brush his.

"Yeah, if it was just my brother – but the two little girls..."

"They're horrible." She could feel his fingers twitch, the anger in his heart. In that moment, she felt what it was like to want revenge. "They're animals, and a big force to be reckoned with. Tell me more about the assignment and how we all walk away."

"I know what needs to be done," he said, straightening, "and originally, this was their plan, but this is my operation. My way now."

"Maybe I can go talk to them. " She thought she was crazy to think she could deal with something this big. She hated the position she had put them all in, over documents.

"You'll get yourself killed. If we did it their way, and you get involved, you get me and yourself in jail, or worse. Do you trust me? Can we do this together?"

"I've been listening and sitting here with this knife in my hand, deciding if I should use it on the guy in front of me, who used me, made me fall in love with him, and then kidnapped me."

"What did you decide?"

"I'm still deciding."

FORTY-NINE

ELLIOT FILLED Ryleigh in, with a lot more details then he had planned to, but she was quizzical and sharp. The hot sun made him sweat. They'd been talking for an hour or so, and he felt a mess, drenched in sweat, and in need of a quick swim and soap.

The more they talked, the more he felt remorse at the possibility of involving Ryleigh deeper than she should be, in his idea and plans. The more he told her, the less he began to think it was a good idea. She looked confused, a bit scared.

"Your mind tells you what it wants you to see. Take the portable bathrooms. Do you remember there were four?"

Ryleigh shook her head knowingly.

"I made sure we had two remain."

"Fuck!" Her gaze at him was stark wonderment. Her emerald eyes were wide.

"And the eggs. Some of the food. Did you ever see me catch the bird?" He released his held breath, knowing his words would haunt her. "Add some of the tiki hut toiletries." He hated the lies as much as she did. There were many times this last month when he'd wanted to cave and tell her.

"That knife you're holding. That's mine. I made sure it was left here."

Her mouth hung open and she gave him the most unforgiving stare. She was mortified. He was in way, way over his head, but it felt so good to finally tell her. Crazy as this all was, he felt she believed him.

Will we ever get through this? Or will this be our end?

"Were you going to kill me? And changed your mind?"

"No! Holy fuck, no, Ryleigh. I did all this for you. I was compromised with the person I was protecting. I got to know you, and my attentions turned to protecting you, too. It's what I do. These are bad people we're dealing with."

Ryleigh nodded. When she looked up, he could see another look in her face. The beautiful woman he had shared the island with for six weeks, who he had frolicked with in the sea, explored the island with, and who he had beaten at Gin Rummy until three days earlier – the love of his life. Tears swelled at the corners of her reddened eyes.

"I don't know what to believe anymore." She had a fleeting look of sincerity in her eyes. *That's my Ryleigh. She's a fighter.*

Elliot gazed at her, tempted to tell all, but he still had work to do.

"I can't tell you everything, but I love my family dearly." He couldn't wait to get ahold of the people who had done this to him, and to his family, his own flesh and blood.

"I know! It's terrible they have someone in your family. That changes so much."

"For your sake, Ryleigh, I really have to keep from telling you more. Think of it as a court hearing. If they called you to the stand, under oath you would have to testify by answering what I've shared with you because we're not married." When he said the word *married*, her face flushed.

"Oh, Elliot, I'm so sorry. Will they come back here?"

He shrugged, desperately trying to act nonchalant, but all he could feel was fear. Fear of losing Ryleigh. Fear of the plan not working. Fear of an operation with so much of a personal side to it.

"I'm not sure who's in charge anymore. But I assure you I have a plan that takes me back to the U.S. Back to Dexco. I will get to the bottom of it. I have the advantage of being on the inside for now."

She winced when he said it.

"We're going to get through this, Ryleigh. After we do, nothing can stop us."

Worry crossed her eyes like a sudden afternoon storm darkens bright skies, and a puzzled frown crept onto her face. "And me?"

He didn't reply. He couldn't give her hope that she would be safe back home. She was safer here than in Chicago, but would this plan work?

A tear slip down her cheek, followed by another.

"Ryleigh, it's not like that." He reached to brush the tear away, but she took a step backwards. He felt a twinge of regret, and of something like grief.

"Well, I'm dead, right? You did your deed."

"If I didn't plan that, they would be after us. We would be the ones being tracked, not the tracker. I'm usually the tracker." His voice had a tone that was nearly a growl of frustration.

"Why didn't we take that chance?"

"Seriously, how would we compete against their thugs here? The Dexco lynch team is well-rested, well-fed, and well-hydrated, not to mention they probably have more than one team assigned to this operation, thus the two boats they sent, waiting on the horizon for my signal."

Ryleigh wrapped her arms across her chest and rubbed her forearms like she was chilled. "What's the new plan? Can you sneak me out? You've got to have someone on the inside that can help us, or help me, get out of here." Her gaze went to the brush on the far side of the beach.

"My plan is for them to keep on thinking you're gone, missing... dead."

"That's the new plan? That you want everyone to keep on thinking I'm dead?" She stood there, lips quivering at him, totally aghast.

"No, not everyone, just Dexco, and any other shithead that is behind my brother's family's kidnapping."

"This works great for you. I disappear to some place far away and take a new name and identity, start a new life. And you get yours back?"

"Oh, no, Ryleigh, this is only until I can uncover them. Expose the mess."

"That's the plan?"

"The best and only way. Do you understand that with Dexco money, and the government resources and teams working in concert with each other, they're almost unbeatable? But I'm one of the best. I have a keen eye, incredible patience, and I know all the signs that I'm being pursued. These signs stand out to me like that neon shirt you're wearing. I can track anyone. I know if sand particles are deposited on a leaf by transference. I can recognize any disturbance in the brush. I could track you easily, if you had a day's head start."

"You're scaring me. All this time I was worried about being stranded, but I have to admit, I was relieved to not look over my shoulder like at home all the time, too." Tears welled in the corners of her eyes again. "You always made me feel so safe. Damn you!"

"You still can feel safe. I'm here still, aren't I?"

"You are so large, and so strong. And me by comparison, I felt so small and weak. You were my hulk man. If I could choose anyone to be stranded on an island with, it would have been you," she whispered tearfully.

He came close to her. She stepped back. "Please–" he tried to touch her arm.

"These chairs we sit on, the sea we frolicked in, and even our straw bed in the hut… this was our world. I felt safe here with you. I felt loved."

She closed her eyes and, when she opened them, she looked so desolate. "So you got us lost that first day? I knew you had something to do with our troubles. I just don't know what to do. Part of me wants to stab you, and another part wants to thank you."

"God, you don't owe me a thanks, but I prefer not to be stabbed."

"I'm struggling to take this all in, to absorb the fact that this absurd isolation was not real, but my mind is a jumble."

"It's all real. We are stranded."

She smiled briefly. "Do you communicate back home? Do you know what's been going on at home?" she murmured.

"No. But I talked a little with the hired pirates. They said the Royal Ahoy ship we sailed on had been hit by high waves in the storm the day it sailed from this area. A lot of people were killed."

Ryleigh cupped her hand over her mouth. "Oh, no. I hope the young girls at our table were okay." She stared into the sand.

"I don't know any details." What he did know was that Dexco thought she was dead, and that was what he had planned to have portrayed.

"Oh, Ryleigh," he whispered. "Please, can we agree to my plan? If I can get back and do what I need to do, then I can come back for you. I've shown you all the ropes. And you'll be safe here."

"Why can't you take me?"

"I have someone that works for Dexco picking me up soon. They have my brother. They would be worried I was going to double-cross them. If the Dexco henchmen see you – game's off. We'll both be dead. And Ron, too, and my nieces."

He could see her veneer crack and sweat formed at her brows. He knew he would do anything to protect his family, and her.

"How long? How long would I stay here? Just long enough for you to overpower their boat and sail back for me?" She smiled a little.

He shook his head. "I have to get back to the States. Then there's the matter of them questioning me about you."

He was half expecting her to lose it after he told her she would be left alone. She edged closer to him and, instead of unraveling, her face began to regain a look of control. "This pathetic plan may actually work."

"Are you agreeing to stay here?"

"It's so crazy," she murmured, shaking her head in a last attempt of denial. "So let me get this straight, there were no pirates?"

"Nope, no pirates."

"But there's still wild animals and snakes?"

"Yes, but we've been fine since I covered the hut with the netting."

"And you planted the playing cards?"

"Yes."

"Okay. I can't believe I'm saying yes." She smiled a shy smile and leaned over and kissed him. "But I still have to believe someone is looking for me."

"I'll find out. Remember the plan."

"All truths, from now forward. Scout's honor?"

"Yeah, about the boy scouts..."

"You were never a boy scout, were you, Hunk-a-berry?"

"No, but does a SEAL count?"

"Will we ever go back to lying? We need to kill it before it kills us." The reminder of all his hidden truths crossed her eyes.

He wasn't sure Ryleigh was trusting his plan.

"We both did it to protect each other. I never doubted your feelings for me, and I hated that my actions and mystery made your

193

heart break." He stared at her, frozen, fear etched on her beautiful face. "There were so many time I wanted to cave. I'm trained not to."

Ryleigh didn't reply.

"Ry, you're scared. I get it. Baby, if I had to do it over again, I'd do the same thing. I never meant to fall in love, but I knew I wasn't going to sit by and let them manipulate me that way, and to take advantage of you, even before I really knew you."

"Was this the only way? I feel so compromised. So corrupted. And I did nothing wrong."

"Remember our plan. We will get even. We'll be freed."

"But this is the government we're talking about." She closed her eyes and shuddered.

"Don't doubt yourself or us. It wasn't us that created this dilemma. We'll get to the bottom of this. God, I felt like I was betraying you, and that tore me up inside." He wrapped his arms around her.

"Why this place? Why did you choose this island?"

"Because of its checkered past, no excursions will come here in the near future."

"There have to be people that already traveled here on an excursion who want to come back?"

"That may be true, some day. For now, because of the ship's accident in these waters, that will keep most away for a while. Before I heard of the ship's catastrophe, before we left on the cruise, Dexco had informed me they knew that R.A.L. would no longer use this island. Nor any other ships due to the shifting sandbars, laborious travel, and it being privately owned, off the maps... this will keep the inquisitive visitors away. And thanks to Dexco, with the help of some high-powered government people, this island has been designated a rare bird sanctuary, and only scientists are allowed here. It will take months to get through all the red tape before they come here again."

"But what about the boats that we came on? They can get past the reefs."

"It's a three hour bumpy boat trip from the nearest port. These islands are ribbons of coral and sand, and this island we're on is a mere spec, poking above the water in the vast ocean. There are dozens in the atoll, two hundred miles northeast of an inhabited village island, which means there's nothing but water between the last cruise stop and our islands here.

"RAL cruises saw these islands as an untapped opportunity to claim unheralded, off-the-grid ports, with no competition. That's why I chose this cruise and ended up on an 850 foot ship, headed to places named Snake Island and Keg Key, destinations that we needed a map of a map to locate."

"Is there any other way? I thought I could do this, here alone, but when the time comes, I'm afraid I'll back out." She gave him a tell-me-I'm-alright expression.

"Ryleigh, you can. You're ready. If I don't go back and do this, sweetheart, you'll be looking over your shoulder the rest of your life."

The yellow bindings on the lawn chair were starting to unravel. She pulled a few off and twirled them in her hand.

"Okay." She handed the knife to Elliot.

He pulled her into his arms. "If we can work through this, then we can work through anything. Okay, partner?"

Ryleigh snuggled close to him. "But–"he stopped her with a tender kiss.

He hugged her tightly and she whispered in his ear, "I know I love you, and I can't change that feeling."

And just like that, the deal had changed. She'd told him she loved him. And he replied back.

"I love you, too. Don't worry," he promised her. "When the time comes, I have an idea for your rescue. I will find you a way home, even if I have to call on the winged-monkeys."

"There's no place like home." She dropped her forehead to his.

"When all is done." Elliot knew it wasn't over. For neither or them, not quite.

FIFTY
Chicago

DETECTIVE CHANDLER glanced around the well-appointed headquarter offices of the global pharmaceutical giant, Dexco. The walls were littered with photos of executives in expensive suits, posing with pill bottles and handfuls of their blockbuster diabetes tablets. He had barely settled into the lobby when the receptionist approached him.

"Mr. Chandler, he can see you now."

"Thanks."

"First door on the left."

Chandler walked a few feet from the lobby, passing a glass conference room door, with an empty table with a dozen leather chairs neatly arranged around it.

"Mr. Greg Edersom, Detective Chandler," he said, walking over and extending his hand to the man standing behind a large mahogany desk.

"Detective, what brings you here?" A confident-looking man in his early forties, jumping straight into the meeting.

What no frothy cappuccinos? No small talk? No relax-the-customer routine? Chandler thought. "Call me Chandler."

"Okay, Chandler, have a seat. I'm Greg." Greg ushered him to a brown high-back chair.

"Thanks." Chandler sat in one of the four chairs, and Greg came from behind his desk and joined him at the table.

"What brings you here? You mentioned on the phone it had to do with one of my employees, Ms. Lane?" Greg wore his graying hair short, in a military haircut, and he was a big man, standing about six foot four inches. He peered at Chandler through tortoiseshell-rimmed glasses.

"Yes, Ryleigh Lane. She works for you?"

"Yes, technically she does. I looked her up, after your call. She reports to the VP of Quality and he reports to me, the Senior VP." He hesitated, then asked, "Is she alright?"

"When was the last time she worked?"

"She had a vacation. I believe a cruise."

"Hmmm," Chandler murmured to himself. "How many employees work here?"

"This office?" The CEO asked.

"Sure," Chandler wondered how a Senior VP reporting to the CEO would know when his employees took a vacation. Greg Edersom not only knew, but he knew where she had taken her vacation.

"To answer your question, we have about twenty-five hundred employees here."

"You're the senior executive of one of the largest companies in the city, and I find it surprising you would know one of your manager's vacation habits."

"We have been concerned, after no one heard from her. She works in quality control and we miss her good work – and her supervisor says it's very uncharacteristic of her to quit in this manner."

"But not impossible?" *Why does Mr. VP think she quit?*

"Of course not. She had been written up lately, and reprimanded for unusual and suspicious activities, not to mention possibly illegal actions. She was on a PIP."

"PIP?"

"Performance improvement plan."

"Not a stellar employee?" That wasn't the image Chandler felt he'd gotten of the lady he was investigating since her ID had shown up inside the dead girl's shorts.

Chandler listened with strained patience to Mr. Senior VP's story. Chandler acted calm when Greg told him Ryleigh was to have been a witness in a class action suit, and how they really had needed her. "Did her family reach out to you all?"

"No, not that I know of, but I can check. There might be a perfectly good reason for her not returning to work. HR called her house number and no one has called back. We fired her after three days of no response, and sent her an email and letter."

"Who called her?"

"HR – I mean, human resources."

"I know what HR is, but who was the person who called her home?"

Greg swirled a black Mont Blanc pen over his computer key pad, then set it down and typed a few words on the keypad. "I believe it would be Christine Kristnas."

"Did you say Chris Christmas?" Chandler on impulse laughed a belly laugh. "Sorry, I just picture a Santa ringing a bell."

"No, I'm pronouncing it wrong probably. It's Christine, and her last name is spelled different than I'm pronouncing it." He smiled a little.

"Do you have her number? I'd like to meet with her."

"She's no longer with Dexco."

"That's a unique… coincidence." Chandler didn't sugarcoat his annoyance with this interview. "Do you know where she is at? Did she leave for a competitor?"

Greg's shoulders lifted in a rolling shrug. "No idea."

"Well, Greg, I appreciate your candor." Chandler watched Greg wince. He'd once been a really good cop, back in the day, and his new P.I. role hadn't ruined his instincts about people and whether they were telling the truth. Mr. Senior VP was hiding something, and maybe even lying.

Chandler left Dexco Pharmaceuticals and was anxious to meet and interview Ryleigh's neighbors in her townhouse building, as soon as he made a few phone calls. He wondered if her milk carton disappearance had left many of her friends wondering where she was.

FIFTY-ONE

THEIR WAKE-UP CALL came early, before the sun came up, from the sounds of a familiar thump-thump-thump of a helicopter's rotary blades.

Elliot rolled over, mumbled something, and buried his head under a stack of bundled t-shirts Ryleigh had made to be used as a pillow.

Ryleigh shot upright. The sounds of a helicopter engine sounded near the beach, and then suddenly all she could hear was the rotary blades above churning, and her heart jumped into her throat. "Elliot, wake up. Wake up." She shook him.

"What, babe?" He sat up and heard the noise, too. "I thought I was dreaming."

"Let's go. Get the fire torch. Holy crap." She opened the door and looked toward the thumping sound. She saw nothing.

She ran to the woods' edge and looked over the dark forest, and Elliot was right behind her. She saw the shadow overhead and then the helicopter vanished out of sight.

"Where'd it go?"

"I think it landed over there." Elliot pointed to the densest area.

"But there's no way. It's so wooded."

"There's an area that is big enough for a landing area. Shhh." They stood in complete silence.

It was unmistakably the purring of a chopper on the island somewhere. But where? And who was it? Were they looking for them?

"I do hear a helicopter," she whispered, standing beside Elliot. "Do you think it's a rescue? Like the Coast Guard?"

"It's a helicopter, but I don't think it's our search party." Elliot whispered to her, squashing the false hope that had buoyed in her.

She raised her gaze to the darkness from the early dawn sky and the canopy of trees overhead. "Let's go find out. Let me grab the shoes." She ran inside the hut and came out with two pairs of shoes. Hers were a pair that they had managed to make out of the rubber flip-flops they'd found in the hut. His were a pair of men's tennis shoes he'd found in the backpack, with the toes cut out because they were too small.

Elliot headed toward the whirling sound.

She followed a step behind him, feeling the euphoria of a potential way off the island. Since the night before, she'd felt a bond, a stronger connection, something new between them, and no more lies, only promises. They'd built their island life together, and that survival instinct made them resilient.

She missed a step and fell against him. "Sorry, it's so dark. I don't care if I run into a nest of snakes, if it means getting off the island." It was dark and the fear raced through her. Her emotions were high after their talks of the plan Elliot had laid ahead for them.

"It's always darkest before the dawn," Elliot said.

FIFTY-TWO

THE LAST THING Elliot wanted Ryleigh to see was what he suspected they'd find at the helicopter. In the darkness, the purring sounds of the chopper in the distance could be heard getting closer as they trudged in the early dawn.

This had been an intense stroke of luck, getting stranded, and time had seemed to slowly tick away, but for now, this idea was as good as it got. It wasn't as planned, but life had taken another turn. How had his strategy been taken by Ryleigh? What would she do? Fate had brought them together and well-laid plans had hit a snag.

"There it is," Ryleigh shouted.

"I see it," he said quietly, with little excitement in his voice. "Looks familiar."

Ryleigh sensed it and stopped dead in her tracks, her heart leaping in her throat, and she covered her mouth with her hand. "No."

Elliot pulled her into his arms. "Be strong. Remember when the time comes, I will always be there."

Tears rolled down her cheeks. Her hand slid out of his grasp. Her body went limp against his. She raised her head, looking out over the dark sky. "Now," she said, gasping.

"You are a woman of wisdom. You are strong. You are ready." He kissed her lightly on the forehead. "Remember our intentions. This will work. I have to do this, to tie up loose ends, to save a lot of people… I'll return." God, this hurt. His eyes filled with tears. Did his plan make sense anymore, or maybe it made no sense at all? The game was on… he would interact normally around his team and people. He knew he would go insane without her at his side.

She didn't reply. She only sobbed and she pressed something into his palm.

With his arms wrapped around her, his mouth met hers, and they sank deep into a long, tearful kiss.

Elliot stepped back, and wiped the hair that fell over her face. "Adieu, Ryleigh, until we meet again." He turned quickly and ran toward the thumping noise. He fought back his own tears. He couldn't stop and look back.

With heartfelt reluctance, Elliot jumped into the helicopter, prepared to help guide the pilot off the island.

"How are the hell are you, Elf?"

"Let's just get out of here."

"This is dangerous," Charlie said.

"Of course, it's dangerous. They wouldn't have hired us if it wasn't." Damn them. "We're clear."

"Yeah, I'll get us out of here. Elf, you've lost a hellava lot of weight. Once we're airborne, I want details. I want to know about the mission, Puff the Magic Dragon."

Elliot hated to be called 'Elf.' He hated the man sitting next to him and he hated the mission they were on. He thought about overpowering the pilot and going after her. But he knew it would be only hours before a new team pursued them. He didn't want to endanger her that way.

"Did you bring her?" Elliot looked around the chopper.

"Yes. She's a beauty. White, female, young–"

"–where is she?"

"Here" The pilot reached behind him and pulled out a large knapsack. "Somewhat trained, plus her natural instincts – all that one does is hunt for food."

Inside, behind the mesh lining, was a white Indian Desert cat, purring to get out. Elliot zipped open the bag and, without a second to spare, he dropped the cat out the helicopter door as they moved slowly off the ground.

"Hey, what the fuck? Why did you–"

"Don't ask. Just leave!" He prayed the so-called stray would find its way to the food he'd hid by the hut.

Without another word, the pilot kept looking at him.

"Can we just get the hell out of here?" Elliot yelled. "What are you waiting for? I said, 'we're clear'."

Hovering over the spot where she could be watching made his wounds hurt even more. Everything blurred as his eyes watered.

After a few minutes, the chopper was airborne, and the shadow he saw in the brush faded slowly away. But the lump in his throat grew larger.

Elliot took the small item from his pocket, a sand dollar, and saw that scribbled on it in pencil was the word *Hunkaberry*. He closed his hand gently around it. *She knew?* He smiled at the smoothness in his palm, careful not to crush the delicate skeleton shell.

He prayed they were good. They could disappear as easily, when the time came. Until then, there was the game to play.

About the Author

This is the first book in the Survival Island Suspense Series. Please visit www.GoPamela.com for other books in the series.

Pamela Laux Moll loves traveling and attributes her creative inspiration to it. Many of her adventures are to remote tropical islands. She lives on an island near Saint Petersburg, Florida. Pamela has published several catalogs, calendars, guide books and novels.

I hope you enjoyed Book One of the Survival Island Series.   In the meantime, if you liked the story, please click below to take you to where you bought it, and write a review, so other readers can hear what you thought of it.

<<link here>>
Or leave a review on Goodreads or Amazon.
Thanks for reading!

Other Books by Pam Laux Moll

Plush	Some Toys You Just Don't Want to Play With
Island of Lies	Survival Island Suspense Series Book 1
Girl Alone on an Island	Survival Island Suspense Series Book 2
Diamond Island	Survival Island Suspense Series Book 3
Sue Me	Previously published as Plush

If you like Book One, *Island of Lies,* please go to www.GoPamela.com and register to receive Book 2 in the Series: Girl Alone on an Island

Girl Alone on an Island

A deadly paradise. A case for the ages. Fighting for her life could mean saving thousands more...

Ryleigh Lane has been stranded on an uninhibited tropical island for over a month. As she waits and hopes for her sexy boyfriend Elliot to return, she must survive the sun-filled days and terrifying nights without him. As the hours tick away, she wonders how soon it will be until the island tremors and treasure hunters end her life.

Elliot Finn feels nothing but guilt for his decision to leave Ryleigh by herself. Doing his best to keep the case against a corrupt pharmaceutical exec alive without its key witness, Elliot learns that the girl he loves may not be as safe as he previously thought.

Surrounded by massive rodents and poisonous snakes, Ryleigh has no choice but to get off the island. Can Elliot get to her in time, or will Ryleigh's luck run out?

Girl Alone on an Island is the second book in the exhilarating Survival Island series. If you like fast-paced action, gripping suspense, and captivating plot twists, then you'll love Pamela Laux Moll's nail-biting novel.

Buy *Girl Alone on an Island* to continue the thrilling series today!

A collectables craze. A deadly secret. Only one woman is willing to fight back.

Sue Logan will do anything for her family. The single mom's startup is her best chance for earning a living, but a secret she learns along the way might put her and her bank account out of business. Everyone Sue knows is obsessed with collecting an extremely popular plush toy. Except the toy could be deadly, and Sue may be the only one who realizes it...

When a billionaire toy manufacturer tries to run Sue out of business, she enlists the help of a shady journalist to save herself and her children. But can Sue trust the reporter long enough to outwit the corporate giant before the unthinkable happens?

Sue Me is a legal suspense thriller. If you like fast-paced drama, strong female characters, and the movie Erin Brockovich, then you'll love this refreshing debut novel from Pamela Laux Moll.

Buy *Sue Me* to collect your next read today!

Note to Readers. Previously Published as Plush.

www.ingramcontent.com/pod-product-compliance
Lightning Source LLC
Chambersburg PA
CBHW051504170626
46811CB00002B/636